D0105106

RAMPAGE WEST

Lew Tune had nothing to do with starting the range war between the Anchor and Spade outfits, but he knew he couldn't remain neutral. If Anchor won the war he would probably be safe, but if Spade came out on top, the small cattle owners would be squeezed out—and that included Lew. Until recently a footloose drifter, he was determined to fight for what he had worked so hard to acquire.

There was also Tracey Fayette, and no amount of danger could discourage him from trying to win her hand. Lew threw in with Anchor, but whilst Anchor had right on its side, Spade had overwhelming might . . .

Leslie Ernenwein was born in Oneida, New York. He began his newspaper career as a telegraph editor, but at eighteen went West where he rambled from Montana to Mexico, working as a cowboy and then as a freelance writer. In the mid 1930s he went back East to work for the *Schenectady Sun*. In 1938 he got a reporting position with the *Tucson Daily Citizen* and moved to Tucson permanently. Later that year he began writing Western fiction for pulp magazines, becoming a regular contributor to *Dime Western* and *Star Western*. His first Western novel, *Gunsmoke Galoot*, appeared in 1941, and was quickly followed by *Kinkade of Red Butte* and *Boss of Panamint* in 1942. In addition to publishing novels regularly, Ernenwein continued to contribute heavily to the magazine market, both Western fiction and factual articles. Among his finest work in the 1940s are *Rebels Ride Proudly* (1947) and *Rebel Yell* (1948), both dealing with the dislocations caused by the War Between the States. In the 1950s Ernenwein wrote primarily for original paperback publishers of Western fiction because the pay was better. *High Gun* in 1956, published by Fawcett Gold Medal, won a Spur Award from the Western Writers of America, the first original paperback Western to do so. That same year, since the pulp magazine market had all but vanished, Ernenwein returned to working for the Tucson Daily Citizen, this time as a columnist. Ernenwein's Western fiction may be broadly characterized as moral allegories, light against darkness, and at the center is a protagonist determined to fight against injustice before he is destroyed by it. *Bullet Barricade* (1955), perhaps his most notable novel from the 1950s, best articulates his vision of how the life of man is not governed by a fate over which he has no control, even though life itself may seem like a never-ending contest against moral evil.

RAMPAGE WEST

Leslie Ernenwein

GUNSMOKE

This hardback edition 2004
by BBC Audiobooks Ltd
by arrangement with
Golden West Literary Agency

ISBN 1 4056 8000 8

British Library Cataloguing in Publication Data available.

Printed and bound in Great Britain by
Antony Rowe Ltd., Chippenham, Wiltshire

THERE was no sign of distant war smoke as Lew Tune rode into Chico Sabino at noon. But the awareness of it, and what it could mean to him, nagged at his mind. This was a time of great turmoil in Mexico—a time of *revolución* with its inevitable aftermath of pillage and rape.

A lean, long-shanked man, Tune looked like a border bum in boots. His black hair shagged long below the brim of his sweat-stained Stetson and his dark cheeks showed a two-day stubble of whiskers. But Tune was no shiftless drifter. Behind him, on the sun-burnished Sonora flats, was his cow camp with a hundred and fifty head of cattle and two Mexican herders.

Chico Sabino wasn't much of a town—just a scatteration of thatched-roof adobes, a general store and the Cantina Flores. It appeared deserted, for this was the traditional hour of siesta. Tune turned in at the cantina, and now a smile altered his high-boned cheeks as he observed a saddle mule and pack burro at the hitchrack. Those two animals were familiar to him; their presence here meant that Keno Smith had returned from his interminable wandering.

So Keno is back, Tune thought, and was wholly pleased. There weren't many Americans in Sonora, and Smith was his only good friend. Even though Keno was some twenty years his senior, they had much in common. They were *simpatico*.

Going into the cantina, Tune grinned at the old man who stood at the bar with a bottle of beer in his hand.

"Think of the devil!" Smith exclaimed, his bearded face creasing into a cherubic smile. "I was comin' out to your camp."

"How did the *pasear* go?" Tune inquired.

"Well, I didn't find the Red Hill yet," Smith admitted. "That's awful big country up around Rosario—bigger'n a Texas barnyard." His eyes, bright as two glass marbles, twinkled, and he added, "But I'll find her one of these days. Just a matter of time is all."

Smith had been searching almost two years for a red hill of copper that had been described by a dying prospector as being in this part of Sonora—a fabulous deposit

5

of ore that would make a man rich if he found it. Keno hunted it with the calm patience of a man courting a lovely woman whose seduction could not be accomplished quickly.

"Let's eat," Tune suggested, escorting his friend to a table and ordering meals for both of them.

Afterward he asked, "Hear anything about the revolution?"

"They say Durango whupped the bejasus out of the *federalistas* at Palo Saba a couple of weeks ago. Which reminds me—your range-leasing deal won't be worth much if the government goes under, will it, Lew?"

"Not worth a plugged peso," Tune said.

While a barefooted Mexican waitress served them, Tune added, "My outfit was started with the winnings from a poker game, so I don't stand to lose much. Easy come, easy go."

It occurred to him that in some ways the past two years had been the best in his life, and the most productive. For the first time he had accumulated more worldly goods than he could carry on his back. Acquisition of property had never meant much to him, he supposed, and wondered why. That reminded Tune of what a girl in Reservation had once told him: "You'll make a lot of horse tracks in the dust, and honey-fuss with a lot of women. But you'll end up a shiftless drifter riding the grubline."

That had started him thinking, but he probably wouldn't have done anything about it if he hadn't made a killing at poker three nights later. Because the girl's prediction bothered him, Tune had put the money into Mexican cattle instead of frittering it away. . . .

Watching Smith wolf his food, Tune thought that Keno hadn't changed much since they had served with the Sixth Cavalry at Fort Apache ten years ago. Smith had been an Army scout then, and before that had trapped beaver in the north country.

Tune, who had been a sergeant then, looked at Smith and marveled that their friendship had lasted so long, or that it had started in the first place. What was it made you like a man, almost on sight, whereas you disliked another man without knowing why? It occurred to Tune that if his father were alive today he would be about Smith's age. But the resemblance ended there, for his father had been cut from an entirely different pattern—a Methodist minister who took pride in being an educated, or as he put it, a civilized and enlightened human being. A smallpox epidemic had left Tune an orphan at fourteen with the necessity of shifting for himself. . . .

They were almost through with the meal when a man hurried into the cantina and collided with the waitress, upsetting her tray.

"That's Bart Hayden for you," Smith cackled. "Always ramming around lively as a lizard hunting a hot rock on a cold morning."

Hayden cursed the waitress, then came to the table and said, "Durango's rebels have taken San Sebastian!"

Tune held a taco in his left hand. He said, "So?" and took a bite, then hoisted a bottle of beer. It occurred to him that he had disliked Hayden from the moment he had first met him.

"You didn't need to be so bitching mean to the girl," Smith scolded. "It wasn't no fault of hers that you come barging in here like a wild jackass with the blind staggers."

Hayden ignored Keno. He said to Tune, "I went by your camp and they said you were here. We've got to get out of Sonora damned fast."

"Shouldn't wonder," Tune agreed.

Perspiration greased Hayden's flushed face and his voice was sharp with urgency as he complained, "You don't seem much interested. This is important, Lew—the *federalistas* are hightailing for the tules right now. A bunch of them came through our place this morning."

"So now the peons take over, and the aristocrats run," Smith chuckled.

Still eating, Tune motioned for Hayden to sit down. "Have a beer," he invited, and calling to the waitress, said, "*Cervesa por mi amigo.*"

Hayden took a chair, and sat poised as if for a quick getaway. He was keyed up with excitement and couldn't relax. "How about you throwing in with us, Lew? With our two herds combined we'd have a chance of running across the line into Arizona."

So that's it, Tune thought. That was why this man wanted to be friendly after two years of standoffish civility.

"How about it?" Hayden urged.

"Maybe," Tune said. "I'd have to think about it."

"What's there to think about?" Hayden exclaimed. "You've got a herd to save, the same as me. Any nitwit knows there's safety in numbers."

Tune made no comment, but finished the taco and used

7

a tortilla to scoop up frijoles remaining on his plate. If he appeared older than his twenty-eight years it was because sun and wind had etched their ancient symbols in his face, for he wasn't one to fret about the future or dredge up past failures.

The waitress brought Hayden's beer, and now Tune asked, "Are you sure about San Sebastian?"

"Positive," Hayden said impatiently. "There were twenty-three *federalistas* in that bunch—the only survivors of the San Sebastian garrison."

So it's all over, Tune thought. He shaped up a cigarette and said, "Well, it was good while it lasted."

"They'll confiscate everything, unless we pull out before they get here," Hayden predicted. Then he asked, "How many cows you got?"

Tune shrugged. "A hundred and fifty, give or take a few head. How many has your pool got?"

"Better than fifteen hundred head. Five years of hard work for four men. By God, we can't let all that go down the drain. We've got to get them out."

When Tune didn't say anything, Hayden said, "I see your two Mexicans stuck with you. Ours didn't. Every damn one of them quit and joined the rebels. You know what that means—they'll lead Durango to our place first thing."

"Shouldn't wonder," Tune agreed, and guessed that Hayden might be regretting his high-handed way with the peons.

"You and your two men, and Keno, along with four of us, could do it," Hayden said.

"Don't count me in on no cattle drive," Smith objected. "I done retired from cowpunching a long time ago."

"But you can't stay in Mexico," Hayden insisted. "Durango is death on gringos. He'll 'dobe wall you sure." Turning to Tune, he asked, "How about it, Lew?"

Tune considered the question, and the man who asked it. He saw Hayden for what he was—an opportunist faced with the necessity of asking for help. Better educated than most cattlemen, Hayden dominated his three pool partners and mistreated his hired help. He hadn't welcomed a fellow American with a government lease two years ago; in fact, he had seemed to resent the competition. But now he wanted to be friendly.

"How long would it take you to get your herd together?" Tune inquired.

8

"One more day," Hayden said. "We've been rounding up for a week."

Tune called to the waitress and ordered three beers.

"But I haven't got time to drink beer," Hayden protested. "I've got to get back to the ranch. How about throwing in with us?"

"Well, if Keno was going I'd say we had an outside chance," Tune said. "But without him I wouldn't hazard it."

"Why not? Keno is just one man—one old man."

"Not so old but what I can fix your piano any day of the week," Smith said, visibly bristling.

Tune liked that. He grinned and said, "I believe you could, Keno."

Then, in the patient way of a man explaining a simple fact to a dunce, he said, "Keno was fighting Indians before you were born, Hayden. He wore out an old 50-caliber buffalo gun about the time you were in knee pants, and a Henry rifle before you were old enough to vote. I'll guarantee that he can shoot farther straighter with a Winchester than any man in Mexico."

"But he's still just one man, one gun," Hayden muttered, and turning to Keno asked, "What will it take to hire you?"

Keno shook his head. "I told you once I retired from cowpunching."

"But you've got your price. Every man has his price. How much?"

Tune said, "I was going to offer him ten steers if he'd help me. Maybe you'd do the same."

"I don't want ten steers," Smith objected. "What would I do with them?"

"Sell for cash in Arizona—if we get there," Tune said.

Hayden wiped his sweat-greased face on a shirt sleeve. He said, "All right, I'll give ten steers."

"How about Ives, Paddock and Engle—would they do the same?" Tune inquired.

Hayden stared at him, his eyes round with wonder. "You mean forty head—just for helping us herd cattle to the border? That's ridiculous!"

"Sort of," Tune agreed. "I can get along all right with my two Mexicans. But I sure won't throw in with your pool without Keno."

While Hayden absorbed that, Smith asked, "What would forty head of steers bring in Arizona?"

"Five hundred dollars or more, depending on the market," Tune said.

Smith considered that in solemn silence for a moment. Then he said, "A man could throw one hell of a wingding in Reservation with that much money. He could stay drunk for six months."

Hayden got up and stood eying Tune with obvious dislike. "A fine thing," he muttered. "Trying to hold up a fellow American, and a friend at that."

Tune's blue eyes showed nothing beyond a passive tranquillity. "Friend?" he asked. "I've heard it said you called me a greasy-sack outfit when I came here two years ago. You've shown me no friendship."

Hayden's ruddy cheeks took on more color. "Is that your final word?"

Tune nodded.

Hayden stood there, his amber eyes revealing the dark run of his thoughts. In this moment he was a big, burly man trapped by indecision—caught between his need for help and his reluctance to pay so high a price for it.

"Maybe you can hire two, three Mexicans cheaper," Tune suggested slyly.

"You know damn well I can't," Hayden said. "they won't work for us—the bastards." He turned to Smith. "Keno, the pool will pay you forty steers."

"*Bueno*," said Tune, as if the issue had never been in doubt. "We'll be ready to roll when you come by my camp."

As Hayden strode angrily out of the cantina, Smith said with mock wonderment, "Why, he forgot to drink his beer."

That was the way it started, with Lew Tune refusing to become excited then, or later when he and Smith rode out to the cow camp and Tune told his two men how it was to be. Old Pancho Gonzales, blind in one eye and showing the scars of a lifetime of hard work, accepted the new state of affairs with a shrug and an open-palmed gesture of fatalistic resignation. But Manuel Robles asked, "What of my wife, señor? I cannot leave her here for the rebels like a plum to be plucked."

"Juanita goes with us," Tune told him. "She can drive the pool chuck wagon."

Then the four men climbed into their saddles and went after the cattle. There was little brush on the flat grass-

"If you want to go along with my drive, all right. But I'll give the orders."

Hayden gave him a squint-eyed appraisal, and the animosity in his eyes matched the restrained anger in his voice when he said, "I'll be remembering this, Tune. I'll remember it real good."

Watching him walk away, Tune thought, *I'll bet you will.*

They ate a leisurely supper without conversation. Even Keno Smith was subdued. The knowledge that *insurrectos* were probably within an hour's ride caused many an apprehensive glance into the darkness beyond the smoldering campfire's glow. Afterward, when the men were lighting up cigarettes, Tune said, "Keno, maybe you'd better ride back and let Ives come in for supper. When the moon comes up, we'll move on."

As Smith faded into the gloom, Tune poured himself another cup of coffee. Observing that Juanita hadn't eaten, he asked, "Waiting for Manuel?"

She nodded.

Frank Paddock asked, "You think they'll come tonight?"

"Probably not," Tune said. "But you never can tell what rebels will do."

Paddock, a mild-mannered man who appeared to be in his late forties, was plainly worried. He said, "If they go back to San Sebastian tomorrow, they'll see our tracks plain."

Bart Hayden was nervous. He kept circling the fire, kept glancing off in the direction Manuel had gone. Finally he said, "Why don't that Mex come back?"

"Give him time," Tune suggested.

Tate Engle and his boy sat together and said nothing. It occurred to Tune that the son was almost an exact duplicate of his short, scrawny father. He asked, "Get enough to eat, Jeddy?"

"Yes, sir," Jeddy said, apparently pleased to be noticed. "I ate aplenty."

Soon after that Manuel rode into camp. When he had unsaddled, Tune asked, *"Insurrectos?"*

"Sí, about fifty of them. Señor Estevan and his *mayordomo* are dead by the patio wall." He made the sign of the cross before saying, "The women are being used by the men, and there is much dreenking—much *celebración.*"

"The dirty dogs," Tune muttered. "Why do they always take out their spite on women?"

13

No one answered him, and now he said, "Maybe we can do something. By God, we can't just sit here while women are being raped."

"What could we do against that many rebels?" Hayden demanded. "They'd make mincemeat of us."

Tune had to admit that Hayden was right. Eight men couldn't hope to win against fifty. But it went against the grain. During his travels he had met up with all kinds of women, some good, some bad, but he had never seen a woman who deserved rape.

"You think they'll spend the night there?" Hayden asked.

"Yes, and maybe most of tomorrow," Tune said. "After that—who knows?"

When the moon came up they shaped the cattle into a trail herd and continued northward.

Moonlight flooded the land so that it was almost like day. The herd, well rested and watered, gave them little trouble. But now, with the threat of pursuit so strong, the drive seemed like a slow-motion procession. Tune issued orders to push the cattle; he rode back to the drag and said, *"Andale, muchachos—push them."*

At daybreak they made a brief halt for breakfast, watered the horses with buckets from a cask on the wagon, and continued on. Tune glanced back occasionally, checking their backtrail, and observed others doing the same. It was a matter of luck, he thought—of how long the *insurrectos* celebrated their raid on Hacienda del Estevan. The knowledge that their fate depended upon the ravishment of Estevan women and the guzzling of Estevan wine stirred up a sense of guilt and futility in him.

At noon they left the grass country. This was flat, barren land—*muy desolado*. If the *insurrectos* jumped them here, there would be no cover at all, and no chance of saving the cattle. The sense of impending attack nagged at Tune now. He glanced back frequently. Late in the afternoon he sighted a dust plume off to the south, and wondered about it. Might be a dust devil.

It evidently was, for at sundown there was no sign of pursuit.

Enough water remained for coffee and for the horses, but Tune cautioned against drinking the small amount left in the cask. "We'll need it about noon tomorrow," he said.

His companions were more confident now. Hayden said, "I think we've given them the slip."

"They're still celebrating at Estevan's," Ives predicted.

"Those boys haven't had that kind of women and wine in all their borned days. Some of them high-toned Spanish women are real choice stuff. Wouldn't mind being with 'em myself."

He evidently had a bottle in his blanket roll for he gave every indication of being half-drunk. Presently he said, "We'll never see them rebels, so we can all relax."

But Tune, knowing the *insurrectos* could cover in one day the distance they had come in two, didn't share his companions' confidence. He let them rest until midnight, then ordered them into saddles.

Red Ives took exception. "Why all the goddamn night riding?" he demanded, "We need some sleep."

"Get on your horse," Tune commanded, and there was something in his restrained voice that made Ives obey without further protest.

At daybreak a hazy row of mountains appeared in the north. Tune squinted his tired eyes, picking out the exact location of San Miguel Pass and aiming for it without stopping for breakfast.

Maybe we'll make it in time, he thought. But the cattle were tired and thirsty now, and so were the men.

Hayden rode up to him and asked, "Don't we stop for breakfast?"

Tune shook his head.

"By God you're being unreasonable," Hayden said. "What difference will one hour make?"

"Might make the difference between saving my cattle and losing them—and yours also," Tune muttered.

"Well, I won't stand for it," Hayden said. "That wagon belongs to us, and it's going to stop long enough for breakfast."

Tired as he was, Tune welcomed this chance for a showdown. Hayden would keep asking for it until he got it, and now was the time. Drawing his pistol he said, "The wagon don't stop, Hayden."

The big man looked at the gun. He said, "Two can play at that game."

"Go ahead and play then," Tune invited, and holstered his gun. "Draw when you're ready."

Hayden eyed him for a long moment while the herd went on. Then he said, "Some other time."

And now Keno yelled, "Look yonderly!"

Glancing back both men saw it at once—a small, yet unmistakable smear of dust to the south.

Two hours away, Tune reckoned. Maybe three.

Ignoring Hayden now, he shouted orders to hurry the cattle. And the men, after one glance rearward, began swinging ropes and yelling.

No grumbling now. No questioning of Tune's orders. The chips were down, and they knew it. They slashed at the cattle, forcing them into a run.

Tune swung over to Jeddy, observing the tight apprehension on his freckled face. "You lead the way with your horses," he said. "Give the cattle something to follow into the canyon."

Then he pulled alongside the chuck wagon and told Juanita to pull up at the north side of the canyon's entrance, and to follow the cattle in.

"*Sí*, Señor Tune," she acknowledged, expertly putting the Spanish mules to a run.

They were within two miles of San Miguel Pass when Tune transferred Engle and Paddock to the point, then took Smith and Hayden back along the trail.

"Rear guard, just like the cavalry," Smith cackled, drawing his Winchester from scabbard.

"How do we manage this?" Hayden asked, his face flushed with exertion and excitement.

"Fan out and watch that we don't get flanked and cut off," Tune said.

He swiveled around for a look at the herd. Under pressure from Manuel and Pancho, it was spreading out some, but that couldn't be helped. And the leaders, following the *remuda*, were close to the canyon's flaring mouth.

In the few minutes, while they waited for the *insurrectos* to come within rifle range, Tune's thoughts reverted oddly to Reservation. Except for that big poker win at Faro Charlie's saloon he wouldn't be here waiting for loot-hungry *insurrectos* to close in. No, that wasn't the real reason either. It was what a girl named Tracey Fayette had said to him—her scoffing denunciation of his aimless mode of living. That, and the fact that he had wanted her as he had never wanted any other woman.

He wondered if Tracey still ran the restaurant in Reservation. . . .

CHAPTER 3

FRANK Paddock swung his rope at the rumps of scampering cattle and yelled himself hoarse: "Hi-ya, cattle—hi-ya!"

They were jammed up at the canyon entrance now. Crowded by riders on both sides and the rear, they were packed shoulder to shoulder, head to tail as they squeezed into the passageway. A calf went down, bawled frantically for a moment, and was tromped into jelly.

When a bunchquitter steer took off to one side, Paddock spurred in pursuit and turned it. He was aware of other riders in the dust-hazed bedlam, and now heard shooting back on the trail as Tune, Smith and Hayden went into action against the oncoming *insurrectos*.

It was hot. Paddock's hard-working horse was lathered, and perspiration greased Paddock's face. But he didn't feel warm. He felt cold, and alone. That seemed odd, because Red Ives and Tate Engle were working near him. But the coldness and the aloneness clung to Paddock like a wet shirt.

He turned a brindle bull that hooked at his horse. "Hi-ya, *toro!*" he croaked and slashed at the bull with his rope.

After what seemed hours, Pancho and Manuel brought up the drags. The two Mexicans were screeching like wild men. A nearly spent bullet whanged past Paddock's head, so close it made him dodge instinctively. Another bullet knocked down the last cow as Manuel came rushing up to hustle her into the canyon.

Ives and Engle had ridden up the sloping sides of the canyon and were yelling at the cattle, while Pancho and Manuel, almost hidden by dust, pushed the drags. The chuck wagon pulled in close behind them.

Abruptly then there was nothing for Paddock to do— unless he joined the rear guard. And he didn't want to do that. Working cattle was one thing, but fighting *insurrectos* was something else. Something he dreaded.

A bullet whined close, and now, with the yelling riders all beyond him, Paddock plainly heard the shooting. He looked out at Tune, Smith and Hayden—and at the *insurrectos*, who were shooting their way forward.

Tune shouted something to him. The distance was too great for Paddock to hear the words, but he knew what Tune wanted. He felt like following the chuck wagon into the comparative safety of the canyon. The urge to follow it was like an ache in his guts. But instead, he yanked his Winchester from scabbard and rode out to the skirmish line. This, he thought, wasn't like hunting deer. This was shooting at men, and being shot at.

When his companions retreated, Paddock did likewise. A slug passed his head so close it made a sizzling sound in his ears. He had turned to fire again when he heard Hayden's yell. Bart's horse was down and the big man motioned for Paddock to come over to him.

The pickup took no more than three minutes to accomplish, but it seemed much longer to Frank Paddock. Bullets kicked up the dust around them as they rode double toward the canyon.

Tune and Smith followed them. When they were in the pass, Tune said, "We make another stand here," and began firing at riders attempting to reach the side slopes.

Red Ives came back, and now Hayden jumped off the horse and fired at an overbold *insurrecto* who attempted to ride up a secondary ridge. Paddock reloaded his rifle, and was almost unseated as his pony spooked at the *insurrecto* who tumbled into the canyon. Blood blossomed like a red flower on the man's face, yet he was attempting to bring up his gun when Keno Smith killed him with a bullet between the eyes.

Paddock wondered about Smith. Keno didn't seem to be frightened. Neither did Tune, nor Hayden, nor Ives. They were sweating, but that was because of the heat, he reckoned. And the excitement. But they weren't afraid. To look at them you would think they enjoyed this.

When he ducked away from a bullet, Keno laughed and said, "The slugs you hear won't hurt you. It's the ones you don't hear that do the damage."

Paddock managed a smile. But he was sick at his stomach.

Tune motioned for them to retreat again. Paddock was wheeling his horse when something smashed against him with a tremendous impact. He thought: *What*—and felt himself falling. After that, for a time, he felt nothing at all.

Red Ives knelt beside Paddock, and examined the wound. "Shot through the shoulder," he said.

Then he joined the others in repulsing *insurrectos* who galloped up the canyon as if intending to ride them down. Robles, Gonzales and Engle came running down the trail to join the rear guard; for a time all seven of those guns kept up a steady firing as the rebels made repeated attacks.

Finally the targets drew back and Tune asked his two Mexicans to tote Paddock to the wagon. "Have Juanita bandage the wound."

As the two started off, cradling Paddock between them, Red Ives called, "There's a bottle in my blankets. Good bourbon. Use a little of it to disinfect the wound."

Hayden and Engle were on foot. Tune dismounted and slapped his horse on the rump, sending it up the trail; Ives and Smith followed suit. The five men backtracked slowly, from one rock reef to another, as the *insurrectos* came at them again and again, screeching like banshees. For the most part they made fleeting targets as they charged through brush and boulders, but some of them didn't live to withdraw.

"They sure want our beef," Hayden muttered, wiping his perspiring face on a shirt sleeve.

"And us," Tune said. Coming to a sharp turn in the trail, he said, "This looks like a good spot to make a real stand. Maybe we can win it right here."

After they had hunkered behind a rock reef and waited for half an hour without another charge, Ives predicted, "We've got 'em licked."

He put down his Winchester and took out a tobacco sack. He was like that, relaxed and confident, when a bullet caught him in the chest.

At this same instant Tune realized that *insurrectos* on foot had managed to outflank his rear-guard position—that they were now shooting from the canyon directly north of them. Bending low, he dragged Ives into a pocket of rocks at one side of the trail. For several moments, while the four of them sent random shots both north and south, they ignored Ives.

"We're in a tight for sure," Keno Smith muttered, seeking a target and not finding one. "Them jaspers must be kinfolk to a mountain goat to get around us."

A bullet bounced off boulders, ricocheted past Hayden and struck one of Ives' legs with a meaty smack. Red yelped a curse, then went into a coughing fit that brought a red froth to his lips.

Tune asked, "You hurt bad, Red?"

Ives tried to answer, and choked. Then he wheezed, "I'm shot through the lung."

His face, contorted by pain, was a death mask. Tune looked at his blood-sogged shirt and said, "Maybe I can bandage it."

"Waste of time," Ives muttered. "What I need—is a drink."

Three mounted *insurrectos* came charging up the canyon. Engle fired point-blank, knocked down a horse, and then Hayden shot the frantically scrambling rider. Tune wounded an *insurrecto* who galloped past the rocks, tilting drunkenly in saddle. The other rebel, a bearded giant of a man, was wheeling his horse in hasty retreat when Keno Smith's bullet caught him. He stayed with his horse for a moment, then, as Smith fired again, toppled from the saddle.

"Come at us some more!" Smith yelled, and shrilled a piercing rebel yell.

For a time then, there was only random firing from hidden guns. . . .

Tune opened Ives' shirt and used his neckerchief to wipe blood from the puckered wound. Red had correctly diagnosed the damage. The bullet apparently had punctured his right lung.

"See that Hayden gives June my share of the cattle," Ives said. He coughed again, and started hemorrhaging. When that was finished, he added, "She lives in Reservation."

"Your wife?"

"Daughter," Ives whispered. A grotesque smile quirked his blood-stained lips. "A looker, like her mother was."

Then, after a pause, he said dejectedly, "I was a hell of a father. Too much bottle."

Tune stayed with him until he appeared to go to sleep, breathing in wheezy gasps.

Bart Hayden seemed not at all concerned with his wounded partner. He kept fidgeting around the rocks on his hands and knees, looking for a target. Finally he asked, "What do we do now, Tune? It'll be dark in a couple more hours."

Tune ignored the question. He glanced at Smith, who had stoked up his pipe and was sprawled comfortably behind a huge boulder. "How many you reckon are above us, Keno?"

"Hard to say, but my guess is not more than four or

five. I don't see how they done it. Them walls are awful steep."

The *insurrectos* were playing it cautious now. They fired occasionally, letting the outflanked men know they were hemmed in, but their bullets bounced harmlessly off the protecting boulders.

"Why don't we rush them?" Hayden asked impatiently.

Tune glanced at Ives, asked, "And Red?"

"He's a goner anyway," Hayden said callously. "If we stay here until dark, they can come through us and then we'll all be goners."

"If you're in a hurry, why, go right ahead," Tune said.

"What are we waiting for?" Hayden asked disgustedly.

"Manuel and Pancho."

Hayden laughed. "You expect those two greasers to get us out of this?"

Tune nodded.

"That's ridiculous," Hayden said derisively. "They're hightailing up the trail, saving their own hides."

Tune shrugged and waited. Some time later he said, "They'll be engaging the rebels about now. When the firing starts, we move in."

But there was no firing for another fifteen minutes, and Hayden scoffed, "Your Mexicans are long gone."

Tune made a cigarette and smoked it. He glanced at Tate Engle, who hadn't said anything—who seemed content to wait and hope. The little man was probably worrying about his son. Tune said, "When the time comes, you stay here and guard Red."

Engle nodded.

The sun slanted into the canyon, its scorching rays cooking a cow carcass just beyond the boulders. The odor became a stench.

The *insurrectos* north and south of them kept up a desultory firing, but made no move to close in. Tune wondered about that, and their willingness to prolong this fight. They had no provisions, and no water save that in their canteens. If they failed to capture the chuck wagon, it would be a dry, hungry ride back to the Rio Felice.

Not all of them, Tune thought, and wondered how many had been killed.

It occurred to him that most of the *insurrectos* had been peaceful peons, working on big ranchos. Men like Pancho and Manuel. They had been *los de abajo*—the underdogs, toiling for frijoles and little else. Some of them had been beaten into submission by the lash of *mayordomos* and all of them had been under the domination of wealthy hacienda owners. Some few, perhaps, had been bandits, but now all of them were *revolucionarios*—sons of the revolt. And they were drunk with the lust for conquest.

Tune thought about Hacienda del Estevan, with its master dead and the women raped. How was it that war could transform men into beasts?

Keno Smith asked, "What you think, Lew?"

"They'll come," Tune muttered. But he wasn't as confident as he had been. Time was running out.

"Those jiggers want our cattle real bad," Smith reflected. "And they want us. You can't blame 'em, in a way. They've been pushed around for years—treated like slaves."

Hayden called, "Are you satisfied, Tune? Do you admit your Mexicans ran out on us."

Tune shrugged, and now, for the first time, became aware of fatigue. The excitement of fighting, with a good chance of winning, had kept him keyed up. But this waiting gave a man too much time to think, and to feel the lack of sleep.

The *insurrectos* north of them were firing again, but now no bullets struck the boulders. Rousing instantly, Tune listened, calculating the distance and guessing that Manuel and Pancho had made their move at last.

"Come on," he growled, and went skulking up the canyon.

The firing continued, the merging reports reverberating through the pass. An *insurrecto* came running down the trail. He ran into the bullet Tune fired at him, and fell headlong. Then a riderless horse spooked past, and soon after that Manuel called, "*Donde esta,* Señor Tune?"

As he and Pancho came warily along the trail, Tune asked, "How many were there?"

"Only four," Manuel said.

Pancho's right arm was bleeding, but he paid it no heed. "We gave them *un golpe terrifico,*" he said gustily.

A terrific smash, Tune translated, and grinned. Going back to the boulders where Ives lay, he said, "We'll tote Red real careful." But when he looked at the sprawled rider, he understood that Ives was dead.

Jeddy Engle worked his way down the canyon, riding slowly past tired cattle that cluttered the trail for more than two miles. Some of the cows had become separated from their calves and had turned about in search of them. Others bawled monotonously for water.

Jeddy wondered what had happened. Why had the herd stalled? Where was the wagon?

The thought occurred to him that his father and the other men might all be dead. Remembering what Manuel had said about the Estevan women, he thought, *The insurrectos may be using Juanita.*

He envisioned how that would be—a dramatic spectacle that both repulsed and intrigued his boyish imagination.

Apprehension was like a tight knot at his throat. If his father was dead, that meant he was an orphan, for his mother had died many years ago. His father had been everything to Jeddy. The thought that he might be dead gave the boy an all-gone feeling that was more than grief— a sense of bewildering panic.

Sunlight had faded from the canyon, and already it was perceptibly cooler. Soon it would be dark. Jeddy tugged his Winchester from its scabbard. Halting his pony, he listened for sound of shooting. There was no sound, save the plaintive bawling of cows.

Perhaps the *insurrectos* were at the wagon, celebrating another victory. Eating and drinking, and having their way with Juanita.

Jerry rode slowly, picking his way through the cattle while doubt and indecision slogged through him. One gun wouldn't mean anything against Durango's rebels. Perhaps he should go back.

But now the cattle had thinned out, and he peered ahead. The canyon was ominously quiet. When finally he saw the campfire, he still wasn't sure—until he glimpsed Bart Hayden's burly form. Hayden was tamping dirt with a shovel at one side of the trail, and Jeddy thought instantly, *Filling a grave.*

Spurring his tired horse, Jeddy blurted, "Who got killed?"

"Red Ives," Hayden said.

Then Jeddy's father stepped forward and asked, "You all right?"

Jeddy looked at his father and blinked through the tears that half-blinded his eyes. "Sure," he said. "Sure I'm all right."

After they had eaten, Hayden and Smith went back down the trail to relieve Tune and Manuel, who were standing guard.

Frank Paddock, who sat propped against a wagon wheel with his shoulder bandaged, said, "Too bad Red had to die."

When Tune and Manuel came to the fire, Paddock asked, "How far do you figure it is to Animas Spring?"

"Another six or seven miles," Tune said. Seeing Jeddy, he added, "I bet your horses are there by now, son. They can smell water a long way off."

"You think the *insurrectos* have gone?" Engle asked.

Tune shrugged. "I think we've licked them, but we'll stand guard tonight, just in case."

There was no night attack. At first daylight Tune warily scouted down canyon and found no sign of *insurrectos*.

They took a beating and toted off their dead, he thought. Returning to camp he said, "We should make Animas Spring before noon and cross into Arizona before dark."

They reached the spring at midmorning, watered the herd and continued on across the broad crest of a ridge. Tune, riding point with Keno Smith, indicated the far slopes and said, "Arizona yonder."

Soon after that Bart Hayden came up and announced, "Once inside Gil Morgan's fence we'll rest the cattle for a few days while I look for some range."

He had been quite subdued, but now showed signs of a revived arrogance.

"You think Morgan will like that?" Tune asked.

Hayden shrugged. "He'll have to—until I find out where we're going."

"Speak for yourself," Tune suggested, and rode on down the ridge ahead of the herd.

Late that afternoon he cut a section of Morgan's fence and pulled the wire back so that the herd could pass through. When the last cow had crossed into Morgan's pasture, he patched the fence.

Now that all threat of another *insurrecto* attack was past, Hayden resumed his domineering ways. He said to Tune at supper, "We'll let the cattle spread out and forget them, while we ride into Reservation."

"We can't spread out here," Tune objected. "This is Morgan's winter pasture. He won't want it all tromped and eaten off by our cattle."

"Well, I'm going no farther until I find some range," Hayden said. Then he added, "Morgan is just a two-bit outfit. He won't squawk very loud."

"He won't squawk about my cows because I'm pulling

out at daybreak," Tune said. "We'll take Keno's forty steers with us."

"You'll do nothing of the kind," Hayden said hotly. "That deal was made under duress. I'll give him ten head —and that's all I'll give him."

Tune put down his plate. He said, "You welching bastard," and slugged Hayden in the face.

The big man teetered back. He wiped his bleeding nose on a shirt sleeve and snarled. "Now you get it, Tune!"

He charged with a bull-like, almost blind ferocity. He took a blow that glanced off his chin, shook his head, and then battered Tune with clubbed fists.

"You smart-alecky son of a bitch!" he raged, and knocked Tune down.

Tune rolled, evading the boot Hayden aimed at his face. He got partway up, was knocked off balance by a second kick and rolled again.

The men ignored their suppers. They watched this in silent astonishment, saw Tune regain his feet and wheel around to clout Hayden with a terrific uppercut to the chin.

"*Bueno!*" Manuel said gustily. And Keno shouted, "Hit him again!"

That blow put Hayden's coordination out of whack. He missed with successive rights and lefts, then staggered drunkenly as Tune clouted him again.

Backtracking now, Hayden was purely on the defensive. Yet when Tune rushed in for the kill, he caught a blow to the head that rocked him immensely. In the moment it took to clear his vision, Hayden attacked again. Moving in close, the big man slugged his lighter opponent with bruising fists, and when Tune ducked away, Hayden snarled, "Stand and fight!"

Tune whirled and caught Hayden with a glancing blow to the head, and as Hayden wheeled sluggishly to face him, got in a jolting right to the midriff. When Hayden's guarding arms lowered, Tune targeted his chin with a solid uppercut that fairly lifted Hayden off his feet.

That did it. Hayden went down and lay there for a moment, groggy and confused. He peered up at Tune as if unwilling to accept the fact that he had been knocked down. He wiped his bleeding nose again, then got slowly to his feet and muttered, "You win—this time."

Panting, and so nearly spent that it was an effort to speak, Tune asked, "Keno gets his steers?"

It took time for Hayden to decide. In this moment, as the big man stood with blood dribbling from both nostrils, Tune understood that Hayden had never intended to pay Keno the forty steers.

"Well?" Tune asked rankly, and squared off as if ready to continue the fight.

"Yes," Hayden said. He turned to Engle and Paddock. "You stay here with the cattle until I get back."

Then he walked to his horse in the uncertain way of a drunken man, climbed into saddle and rode off toward Reservation.

Watching him go, Paddock said, "I ought to have this wound looked at by a doctor."

"You can ride in with me in the morning," Tune suggested.

"But Bart said to stay here."

Tune peered at him. He asked, "Do you always do what Hayden says?"

Paddock thought about that for a moment before saying, "Well, he runs the pool. We—there has to be a boss."

Tune felt ashamed for him. He said, "Suit yourself," and poured a cup of coffee.

When they had resumed eating, Engle said, "I don't reckon Frank and me begrudge Keno his steers. He earned them."

The next morning all cattle bearing Tune's Big T brand were cut out and shaped into a trail herd, plus forty pool steers. Tune said good-bye to Paddock, Engle and Jeddy, wishing them well. Then the three men and Juanita started off with the cattle and six extra horses.

Tune cautioned Juanita to ride slowly, guarding against a miscarriage.

"Sí, Señor Tune," she agreed smilingly. "I weel ride weeth care."

They went out through a pasture gate into the road to Reservation, after which Tune said, "I'll go ahead and see what I can do about leasing some range."

"Take a drink for me at Faro Charlie's," Keno suggested.

Riding toward town, Tune felt good despite a soreness along his ribs where Hayden had kicked him in last night's fight. This was another day. There was a good chance he could find graze for his cattle with an old friend, named Jim Beam. If Jim wasn't overstocked, the cattle could be put on his place at least until other arrangements could be made.

Tune wondered if Tracey Fayette was still in Reservation and hoped she was. . . .

Near noon he met Gil Morgan coming from town in a wagon.

"I camped overnight in your pasture," Tune said. "My herd is coming back yonder."

"I saw Hayden last night," Morgan muttered. "He as much as told me his cattle would stay there until he gets ready to move them." A slow-talking man who'd been a farmer in the Middle West before coming to Arizona, Morgan said, "I explained that it's my winter graze. I told him he'd have to move them soon."

"Did he agree?" Tune asked.

Morgan shook his head.

"I didn't want to start a fuss with him, Lew. There's already too much trouble around here with Spade and Anchor fixing to fight."

He looked at his big-knuckled hands and added, "But I felt like giving him a piece of my mind. He's a brash one, that Hayden."

"That he is," Tune agreed, and rode on.

Morgan had never been overly friendly the few times Tune had met him. The man was somewhat of a loner, and a non-drinker, Tune guessed. But being unsociable didn't lessen his rights to save winter pasture for his own cows.

Presently he got to thinking about Tracey Fayette and how good it would be to see her after two years. She was all woman, Tracey—built the way a woman should be, full-bosomed, yet with a supple, leggy slenderness that made her appear taller than she was. He guessed her age to be about twenty-five.

Old enough to have some sense, Tune thought.

Too much sense, where he was concerned. Tracey had recognized him for what he was: a footloose man with no thought of matrimony.

"I'm not impressed by your blarney," she had told him.

Tune grinned, remembering how calmly she had repulsed his more romantic advances. She knew how to handle a man. Thinking back, Tune wondered why she hadn't married. Tracey had never lacked for suitors, yet she kept them all at arm's length in a good-natured way. She was no prude, certainly; in fact, she was quite frank in discussing the aspects of man-woman relationships. But apparently she was wholly self-sufficient.

Her background, Tune had learned, was similar to his

own. An orphan, she had come to Reservation to live with a widowed uncle; when he died she had used her modest inheritance to buy the Acme Restaurant, which she operated with the dedicated intentness of a person who cherishes an opportunity to be independent.

Tune couldn't blame her for that. Frontier cowtowns were difficult for women with no means of support. A good-looking female had three choices—to get married, to take a poorly paid job as a waitress or turn prostitute.

It occurred to him that Tracey would be good at any of the choices, if she put her mind to it.

CHAPTER 4

AT the edge of town Tune looked ahead and decided that Reservation hadn't changed at all. There was the same scatteration of cattle pens and chutes at the west end, with Fancy Mayme's parlorhouse directly across the road. As he passed the two-story frame house with its shuttered windows, Tune was amused at the thought that it looked perfectly respectable in this day's bright sunlight. But come dark, with red lamplight showing at the parlor window, it was a man-trap promising rowdy diversion for footloose men.

Beyond Mayme's place was the cemetery with its sagging picket fence and weed-grown graves. A few headstones were in evidence, but there were many more wooden crosses, some of which were fairly new and painted white while others were scoured by long exposure to the elements.

Less than a quarter of a mile farther on, the road became a street with twin rows of business establishments—a hodgepodge of false-fronted frame and brick buildings in varying degrees of dilapidation. None was new, and some appeared in the last stages of deterioration with sagging stoops and tip-tilted board awnings. But they all looked familiar to Tune and the sight of them gave him a good feeling. He had been homeless all his adult life; this town was as near home as any he had ever lived in.

There was Green's Feed Store, the Wells Fargo wagon-yard and the blacksmith shop. When he passed Hanley's Barbershop, Tune thought, *I need a shearing and a bath.* But he rode on toward Faro Charlie's Saloon. Charlie would probably be able to tell him what he needed to know —if Jim Beam still had his homestead in the Hoodoo Hills and how many cattle he was running.

They had been good friends. In fact, he had tried to talk Beam into throwing in with him on the Mexican deal. Beam's bachelor camp didn't amount to much, being merely a shack and some forty-odd cows when he had last seen it. But Beam was the steady-going, plodder type, and he had a case on Tracey Fayette.

Him and a dozen others, Tune thought amusedly.

Passing Tracey's Acme Restaurant now, Tune peered at the place, hoping for sight of her. The front door was open, and a menu was pasted on the window, so he thought, *She's still here*. The building, a converted mansion that had once been the home of a wealthy pioneer, had recently been painted. Its white with blue trim seemed out of place among the weather-beaten structures on the street.

As Tune passed the Palace Hotel two old men sitting on the veranda gawked at him, and one of them called, "Things get too hot for you in Mexico, Lew?"

Recognizing Jake Steinheimer, who owned the hotel, Tune nodded. Bart Hayden, he guessed, had spread the news. Thinking of the forty steers Keno Smith had collected, Tune chuckled. Keno would have a spree for himself with the proceeds from the steers—a real hellbinder of a spree.

When he turned in at Pelky's Livery Stable, Tune looked at the little derby-wearing man in the doorway and asked, "Want to buy a good horse?"

Miles Pelky, who wore a pair of steel-rimmed glasses low on his nose, peered over them and inquired, "Is it the one and only Lew Tune, or do my dim eyes deceive me?"

They shook hands in the manner of old friends, and as the liveryman led Tune's horse toward a stall, Tune invited, "Come have a drink with me."

"Too early in the day," Pelky said. "I'm on the wagon —sunup until sundown."

"Since when?" Tune inquired.

"Since I woke up in Mayme's place and didn't even remember going there," Pelky muttered. "When it gets like that, it's time to cut down."

Tune grinned and walked along the street to Faro Charlie's Saloon. There was the same gnawed hitchrack in front of the place and the same litter of horse droppings. Even the two horses tied there had a familiar appearance, for they wore Anchor brands. Recalling all the poker games and Saturday night fun in this saloon, Tune chuckled. It was good to be back.

Entering the saloon, he identified its two customers as Tilt Isham and Whitey Melotte. Isham, ramroad of Anchor, was an important man in this part of the country. Melotte, younger and bantam-sized, was his straw boss— or, as the malcontents put it, "Isham's enforcer." They stood at the bar, a bottle before them, while Faro Charlie sat with his feet propped up on a deal table, reading a copy of the Tombstone *Epitaph*.

"So you're back," the saloonman muttered, peering over the top of the paper. There was a plain note of rebuke in his voice, and an expression of mild reproach on his heavy-jowled, unsmiling face.

As Charlie started to get up, Tune said, "Don't move on my account. I don't want a drink—just information."

"Such as what?" the big saloonman inquired.

"Has Jim Beam still got his place in the Hoodoo Hills?"

Instead of answering, Charlie glanced at Isham and asked, "Has he, Tilt?"

"Well, his place is still there, but Beam is missing," Isham said.

And Melotte added, "Maybe he won't be back."

"Why not?" Tune asked.

Melotte looked at Isham, said, "You tell him, Tilt."

The tall ramroad poured himself a drink, seeming in no hurry to talk. He lifted the glass and contemplated its contents for a moment before gulping the whiskey.

Sensing that something was wrong here, Tune turned to Charlie and asked, "What is it—some trouble?"

The saloonman said, "Well, Anchor tried to buy Beam out. But he refused to sell. Then, according to Anchor, Beam was caught slow-elking Anchor beef."

"I don't like the way you tell it," Isham said, not critically, but in the way of a man wanting to set a record straight. "It sounds like Anchor jobbed him, and that's not right."

"Then you tell it," Charlie suggested.

"Well, there is absolutely no connection between Beam's refusal to sell and the accusation of rustling," Isham said, addressing his words to Tune. "A matter of months separates the two incidents, and one has nothing to do with the other."

Faro Chalie asked, "Has the fact that Beam's homestead

lies between the Spade outfit and Anchor anything to do with it—and the fact Spade is giving Anchor fits?"

Isham shook his head.

Tune remembered him as an easy-talking, rather jovial man. But now he seemed reluctant to speak, which was odd.

"Has Beam been run off his place?" Tune asked, trying to make some sense to all this fragmentary information.

"I wouldn't say that," Isham said. "We went looking for Beam and found him gone."

"What did you expect—that he'd stay for a hanging?" Charlie asked disgustedly. "Jim Beam ain't overly bright in some ways, but he ain't exactly a dunce."

Isham contemplated the saloonman for a moment, his long, high-beaked face wholly grave and a sharp appraisal in his dark eyes. Finally he said, "Sometimes I wonder about you, Charlie. Sometimes I think you're not overly bright either."

Then he walked out of the saloon, his spurs setting up a measured tinkling to his sauntering departure.

Melotte followed him to the doorway, where he turned and said, "Better not tie in with Beam, Lew—or you might get in a bind."

As Melotte went out, Tune asked insistently, "What's this all about, Charlie?"

The saloonman shrugged. He passed a big, tallow-white hand over his balt pate and muttered, "Spade and Anchor are working up to a big fight. Beam got caught between them. They've both tried to buy him out. Finally Anchor jobbed him, pure and simple."

"But old Mike Cavanaugh isn't that kind of a man," Tune objected.

"Mike died a year ago. Anchor is owned now by heirs who live in Chicago."

"So that's it," Tune mused. He thought about it for a moment and then said, "I didn't think Tilt Isham was that kind of man either."

Faro Charlie shrugged again. "Maybe Tilt has got too big for his britches, being practically his own boss and all. I understand he's getting paid a percentage of the profits, in addition to his salary. Tilt has a good thing now. Better than when old Mike was alive."

"I still don't think he'd frame a man cold," Tune said.

"Maybe Whitey Melotte did the framing, without Isham's knowledge."

"Why would Whitey do that?"

"Well, he's got quite a case on Tracey Fayette, who seemed to prefer Beam's company. A little guy like Melotte would resent that. He'd hate Beam's guts."

"How long has Jim been missing?"

"About a week." Getting up now, Charlie propelled his huge, aproned bulk behind the bar and invited, "Have one on the house."

Tune nodded. Acutely worried about Beam, he asked, "Any idea where Jim is?"

Charlie shook his head. "There's lots of places in the Hoodoos where a man can hide out. And there's plenty of greasy-sack nesters who'll feed him. They have no reason to love Anchor."

"Is Spade trying to crowd in on Anchor again?" Tune asked.

When Charlie nodded, Tune said, "They had trouble about ten years ago, didn't they—some shooting, wasn't it?"

"Lasted damn near a month," Charlie said. "Anchor lost two men and Spade lost five, counting Tom Greer, who got so badly crippled he ended up washing dishes at the Acme. Nobody won, but it put a real crimp in Spade."

They had their drink, and then Charlie said, "The trouble between the two outfits goes back to when Riley Cameron and Mike Cavanaugh were partners. It was the Double C in those days. But they were different breeds. Mike was ambitious, but he was scrupulously honest. A real man in every department. Riley was on the shady side, a conniver who'd do anything to get ahead. They split up. Mike had more money and spread out bigger than Riley, who resented it. He couldn't abide Anchor being so big."

"Why do both outfits want Beam's place?" Tune asked.

"Water. Jim has a good spring. If Anchor got it, they could use a lot of their west range that's dry as a bone. Spade doesn't need it that bad, but if Cameron had it he could crowd Anchor some—which would please him."

Charlie poured another drink, and Tune paid for it. Then he asked, "Where'll I put a hundred and fifty cows, Charlie? They're due at the pens tonight, or in the morning."

"Well, you could just throw 'em into the Hoodoos and hope you don't get rustled blind. Or you could put 'em on Beam's place. I guess Jim wouldn't mind. He ain't got many cows of his own."

Tune thought about that, then asked, "Do you know if Bart Hayden leased range for his cattle?"

"He made a deal with Spade," Charlie said. "I wouldn't be surprised if they throw in together against Anchor."

"That'll make a partnership," Tune muttered. "Two first-class connivers. They'll cheat each other blind." Then, thinking of Paddock and Engle, he said, "Bart's two partners probably won't like associating with that Spade bunch, but they won't do anything about it."

CHAPTER 5

TRACEY Fayette was sitting at a table, working on the next day's menu, when Lew came into the Acme. There was no one else in the restaurant, for it was after three o'clock now.

"Am I too late for a noon meal?" Tune inquired politely.

Tracey gave him a momentary appraisal, a half-smile altering the contours of her oval face. She said, "The man looks a little ga'nt, but otherwise he hasn't changed much."

Then she got up and held out both hands and said, "Lew, it's good to have you back."

Tune took her hands. He asked, "Do I get a hello kiss, ma'am?" and not waiting for an answer, took her into his arms.

He didn't kiss her at once. He looked at her in the way of a man savoring a long-anticipated treat. "Your eyes are the same shade of powder blue," he mused. "And the bridge of your nose is still dusted with freckles—little-bitty ones."

Locked in his arms, Tracey protested, "Someone might come in, Lew."

That amused Tune, for it was so like her—always worrying what other people might think. There was a Puritan streak in her that was in conflict with womanly impulses and appetites. "If we're seen, you'd have to marry me," he jeered, and shouted, "Come see what I got, folks!"

Tracey tried to tug free, whereupon Tune took his kiss— a hungry, demanding kiss that had been two years in the

33

making. When he realeased her, they were both a trifle breathless.

Tom Greer, a nonedescript man with a wooden peg for a left leg, stood in the kitchen doorway. He asked, "What's going on?"

"Nothing," Tracey assured him, her fingers busy re-arranging her high-coiled sorrel hair. "It's just Lew—announcing that he's back."

Greer glanced at Tune, said, "Hello, Lew," and went back to the kitchen.

"The cook is off till four o'clock, but I can fix you something," Tracey offered.

"Whatever you have that's ready—anything at all," Tune said.

While Tracey went to the kitchen, he sat at a table and marveled that he should be here. *I can thank Durango for this*, he thought, and was genuinely glad to be back. Tracey hadn't changed at all; she was still the finest woman he had ever known.

When she brought his meal, Tune looked at the warmed-up beef and home fried potatoes and said, "Smells good enough to eat."

Tracey brought him coffee and then sat opposite him, observing that even though he was obviously hungry, he didn't wolf his food as some men did. He needed a shave and a haircut, but he didn't look trampy. There was something about him—a look of class—that distinguished him. Even needing a bath, as he most certainly did, he still didn't look like a saddle bum.

"Is your herd arriving today?" she asked.

"Tonight, maybe. Keno Smith and two Mexicans are trailing them in."

There was another long silence, then Tracey reflected, "It seems odd that you own cattle. I never thought you had that much ambition."

"Me neither," Tune admitted. "But something a girl said to me once got under my skin."

"What?"

"Well, this girl said I was a shiftless, no-account tramp making horse tracks in the dust. She said I'd never amount to anything."

Tracey blushed. Her capacity for schoolgirl embarrassment despite an adult accumulation of worldly wisdom tickled Lew Tune. It enhanced her womanliness, giving her a feminine charm that made her the more desirable.

She said, "I didn't think you'd ever own cattle."

"But I've got 'em—a hundred fifty head. Aren't you proud of me?"

Tracey nodded. "Proud and astonished."

Remembering his promise to look up Red Ives' daughter, Tune asked, "Do you know a June Ives?"

"Yes, and so do you, only her married name was June Patterson."

"You mean the redheaded waitress that used to work for you?"

Tracey nodded, whereupon Tune grinned, recalling the flirty young widow whose husband had drunk himself to death. "Is she still in Reservation?"

"Yes, but not waitressing. She graduated to Fancy Mayme's place. Why do you ask?"

"Her father stopped a bullet on the way out of Mexico. Before he died he asked me to look her up."

"Well, she's not hard to find," Tracey said, obviously resenting his interest in the ex-waitress. "I hear she's the belle bawd of the whole shebang out there."

Tune laughed at her. "You sound jealous," he teased.

"Jealous! How can you say such a thing?"

"Well, you act like you didn't want me calling on her," Tune said, immensely enjoying her womanly anger.

"Why should I care, one way or the other?" Tracey demanded.

She held up her left hand, showing him the small diamond ring on her finger.

Tune stared at the ring. "You're engaged?" he asked in disbelief. "Who to?"

"Jim Beam."

Tune gave his attention to shaping a cigarette. "Don't suppose I should be surprised," he said slowly, as if thinking this out as he went along. "But I am. It just never occurred to me that you'd accept Jim as a husband. I thought you were waiting for someone real special."

"You, for instance?"

She had this faculty for directness—for asking questions that placed him on the defensive. Tune had never resented it before, but he did now.

Presently he said, "I hear Jim is in trouble."

Tracey nodded. "Poor Jim. All he's had is trouble. Last year he practically went broke buying an expensive blooded bull which proceeded to get colic and die. In January he broke his arm. And now this."

"You don't think he slow-elked an Anchor beef, do you?" Tune asked.

"Of course not. That hide with the Anchor brand was planted on Jim's place to give them an excuse to drive him off. They even told it around they were going after him, so someone would tip him off. They wanted him to run."

Faro Charlie came barging into the restaurant and announced, "Lew, your crew has been shot up."

"Shot up?" Tune echoed.

Panting from exertion, Charlie said, "Gil Morgan just drove into town with two dead men, a dead woman and Keno Smith. Keno is shot in the head, but he's still alive."

Stunned, Tune stared at the saloonman in speechless astonishment for a moment before demanding, "You mean somebody killed Juanita?"

Charlie nodded.

"But she's a girl!" Tune exclaimed. "And she was going to have a baby."

Then he got up and started for the doorway.

"Keno is at the hotel, and Doc Snyder is with him," Charlie said, following Tune outside. "Morgan took the others to the undertaker."

The news was spreading fast. A crowd was gathering in front of the Palace Hotel when Tune rushed inside and demanded, "What room is he in?"

"Number three," Jake Steinheimer said. "Any idea who did it?"

Ignoring the question, Tune hurried upstairs.

Keno Smith lay unconscious on a bed while Doctor Synder used a damp cloth to wash blood from a wound high on his left temple.

"How bad is he?" Tune demanded.

"Can't tell yet," the doctor said. "Concussion, certainly. Maybe a fractured skull."

Keno's face was ashen, and for the first time since Tune had known him, he looked old. Really old.

As the doctor finished his examination and began bandaging the wound, Smith groaned and opened his eyes. For a moment he could not focus them properly; he kept blinking his eyes as if Tune's image was fuzzy and remote to him. Finally he said, "We—got—raided."

"Better not try to talk now," Tune said. "Just take it easy."

Keno kept staring at him unsmilingly. He said, "We didn't have a chance, Lew."

Then he closed his eyes and appeared to sleep.

"What do you think, Doc?" Tune whispered.

The physician shrugged, said, "If he's rational when he wakes up, it's probably just a concussion."

CHAPTER 6

LEW Tune had seen his full share of sudden death in the cavalry and afterward, while drifting along the border country. He had seen comrades die, and been saddened by their passing. But Juanita's death was different. It shocked him completely.

He was sitting beside Keno Smith's bed when Tracey Fayette came into the room and said, "I'll watch him while you eat supper."

Tune looked at her. As if repeating an all-important question, he asked, "Why did they have to kill Juanita?"

Tracey had never known Tune to be less than cheerful—a man who took his luck, good and bad, with a shrugging fatalism. She had considered him shallow in that respect, recklessly disdainful of consequences.

Puzzled by Tune's inability to accept the Mexican girl's death, she asked, "Had Juanita been with you a long time?"

"Only since she married Manuel. But she wanted to have a baby. When we started the drive, Juanita said she was glad the baby would be born in the United States—that he would never be a peon. She was sure it was going to be a boy."

Tracey said wonderingly, "You place a great deal of importance on motherhood, don't you, Lew?"

When he didn't answer, she reflected, "I never imagined you did. I thought you looked on women as—well, as quarry to be chased."

Tune shaped a cigarette and lighted it. Dully, as if expressing a question that wholly baffled him, he asked, "Why did they have to kill Juanita?"

"It's horrible," Tracey said. "But you know how some men are—they think Mexicans don't count, men or women."

Tune smoked in moody silence for a moment. Then he said, "They were herding my cattle. I feel responsible."

"But it's not your fault," Tracey insisted. "And you

shouldn't blame yourself. Go get a drink. I'll watch Keno until Mrs. Ledbetter comes."

"Mrs. Ledbetter?"

"She's a practical nurse—helps Dr. Snyder with his patients."

Tune glanced at Smith. He said, "Keno's color is better. Maybe it's only a concussion."

Then he left the room.

When the saloon closed at midnight, Faro Charlie escorted Tune, staggering drunk, back to the hotel and put him to bed.

Juanita, Manuel and Pancho were buried the next day. Tune attended the funeral in scowling, tight-lipped silence, his anger more apparent than grief. Afterward, when Sheriff Jeff Dixon reported that no trace of the rustlers had been found, Tune said angrily, "I'll find Bart Hayden and I'll kill him."

Dixon didn't like that. His age-mottled face was entirely grave as he said, "You'd better have absolute proof before you kill anyone, Lew—legal proof that will stand up in a court of law. Otherwise you'll be in trouble."

"I'm in trouble now."

"But not with the law. Hayden spent all yesterday at Spade, and has Riley Cameron for a witness. I'm convinced that Hayden's two partners didn't leave Gil Morgan's pasture."

"How about Spade's crew?"

"According to Cameron they were working the north range around Chico Arroyo all day. I've had two deputies out looking for your cattle. The trail led into the Hoodoo Hills."

It occurred to Tune that Dixon had always been considered a big-outfit sheriff—that he straddled the fence between Spade and Anchor while dispensing strict law enforcement among the small ranchers and homesteaders.

"I'm not concerned with finding the cattle," Tune said. "It's the killers I want to corral."

"When Keno Smith regains consciousness he may be able to tell something that will give us a line on the killers," Dixon said.

An hour later Tune saddled his horse at Pelky's Livery.

Watching him cram provisions into his saddlebags, Miles asked, "Going hunting?"

Tune nodded.

"Them hills are full of Spade and Anchor riders fussing for a fight," the little liveryman warned. "Trigger-happy galoots just looking for targets."

"I'm looking for targets myself," Tune said, and rode out of the barn.

He passed the cemetery, seeing the fresh-filled graves and cursing morosely.

When he came to Fancy Mayme's place, he dismounted and knocked on the door. There was no answer, so he knocked again, banging on the door with insistent force.

A woman stuck her head out an upstairs window, said, "We're closed until four o'clock."

"Tell June Patterson I want to talk to her," Tune said gruffly. "It's about her father."

The woman went away. In a few moments June Patterson came to the window, sleepy-eyed and tousle-haired.

"Hello, handsome," she greeted, leaning out the window so that her ample breasts were partially exposed above a flimsy kimono.

"Your father got killed in Mexico," Tune said. "He asked me to tell you that you've inherited his share of the herd Bart Hayden brought out."

"What's his share?" June asked, obviously not interested in the fact her father had died.

"More than three hundred head."

"Why, that's wonderful news!" June exclaimed, smiling at him. "I never dreamed my old man would leave me anything. I haven't seen him for a long time, and didn't care if I never saw him again."

"You won't," Tune said.

"Where are the cows?" she asked, a plain note of possessiveness in her voice.

"In Gil Morgan's pasture," Tune said.

Afterward, riding along the road at a trot, he thought, *Poor Red*. Ives' daughter didn't miss him. All she was interested in was her inheritance—the cows that had cost Red his life.

It occurred to Tune that if anything happened to him there wouldn't even be a daughter to inherit his cattle.

What cattle? he thought derisively.

As of right now he was back where he had started two years ago, with no more worldly possessions than he could carry on a horse. And because Tracey Fayette was engaged to Jim Beam he had less.

Then Tune remembered Faro Charlie's report that nine of his horses had been brought in, four of them saddled. So he had that much to show for two years in Mexico.

Nine horses.

CHAPTER 7

TUNE'S cattle had left a broad trail that angled northward from the Reservation Road. They had been driven by three men, according to the horse tracks—one rider ranging back and forth and pushing them from the rear, the others on each side.

Three men.

Three killers, Tune thought, and cursed them in the sighing fashion of a man mouthing a litany.

There were two sets of fresher horse tracks close together which he guessed had been made by Dixon's deputies.

Tune resisted an urge to put his horse to a run. There was no telling how long this would take, and he didn't want a played-out pony at the end of it.

The land lifted gently on this long slope that led to the Hoodoo Hills. The cow tracks snaked around mesquite thickets and across dry washes; the soil, which had been soft adobe. gave way to flinty expanses of rock-littered earth. Finally the trail tilted up the first ridge, dipped through a brush-tangled arroyo, and then rose again through a series of rock reefs festooned with chaparral.

Afterward, as the trail gained more elevation, the mesquite was replaced by live oak; late in the afternoon Tune passed through a skimpy stand of pine.

Near sundown he watered his horse at a seep and refilled his canteen, then continued riding until the trail was no longer visible. It was twilight when he made a dry camp in a high saddle where there was grass for his horse.

Tune built a fire, then sliced three slabs of bacon into a skillet. He sat moodily, watching the bacon fry as full darkness settled and a cool breeze came off the higher ridges. This was the tag end of summer, with the first hint of fall's chill evident at this altitude. In another month it would be cold at night up here.

He poured water from his canteen into a battered coffee-pot and placed the smoke-grimed container on the coals.

This, he thought dismally, was what happened to a footloose man who got ambitious—a lonely campfire in the hills. Bacon, bread and coffee.

Remembering the manner of his becoming ambitious, Tune's firelit face creased into a bitter, self-mocking smile. He hadn't exactly expected Tracey Fayette would marry him, nor had he especially wanted to get married. But the thought was there, as something that might occur in the future. Yesterday, seeing her again, the thought had turned into a high, brief hope. Never before had Tune admitted, even to himself, that the possibility of marrying Tracey Fayette had been the motivating force behind his ambition. But he admitted it now, and felt something close to shame. A man should be the master of his own fate; he should choose his mode of life, doing what pleased him. No woman should tell a man how to live, Tune thought. But Tracey had prompted him to turn from his easygoing habits. Her scoffing remarks had caused him to buy cattle—to be something other than a footloose, easy-riding man.

And what had it got him? Trouble. Death for Juanita, Manuel and Pancho.

Tune ate his sorry supper without relish and sat gazing into the dying embers of his fire until it turned to ash. Then he untied his blanket roll, tilted his saddle so that its sheepskin lining made a pillow, and went to sleep.

Up before daylight, Tune built his fire and used its flickering light to prepare a frugal breakfast. He had slept fitfully, awakening with obscure fragments of bad dreams; once he awoke clutching his pistol and had dredged up part of a dream in which Jim Beam seemed to be shooting at him.

Tune was riding at dawn, his leather jacket tightly buttoned against the morning chill. There wasn't a cloud in the sky; as soon as the sun rose it began warming up. Warily watching the trail ahead, Tune recalled his last trip through these hills, while working roundup with Anchor. That was three years ago, and Spade had thrown in with them to work the Hoodoos, which formed a long southern barrier to both ranches. Not many Anchor or Spade cattle ranged these high roughs where three or four nesters ran their greasy-sack outfits on the scant graze.

This is where I'll probably end up, Tune thought. Providing he found some of his cattle . . .

Shortly before noon he observed what he supposed were the two deputies' tracks, angling off the trail toward the southeast. Apparently they were heading back to Reservation, and he wondered what they had learned. Two hours later Tune found something that puzzled him. According to the tracks there had been a temporary holdup here, one bunch of cattle going west, another going east, and still a third bunch heading north.

This was a comparatively flat stretch of country lightly timbered with pine trees. Deciding to scout the east trail, Tune rode for upwards of an hour before coming to a grassy pocket where he counted thirty-eight head of his cattle—mother cows with calves, a few steers and a bull. All of them were gaunt, showing signs of hard travel.

Why had the rustlers diverted this bunch?

Unable to figure it out, Tune went back to the holding ground, then scouted the west trail to where it petered out on an expanse of black malpais that extended as far as he could see. There were no tracks to follow here; only the occasional scar of a shod hoof or cow droppings. After his bay pony had clattered over the flinty rock for a mile with no sign, Tune circled south without finding a trace of travel.

Finally giving up, he went back to the main trail and followed it north, climbing into a region of barren, rocky ledges. Again he had trouble, discovering only occasional tracks and failing to find where the cattle had been turned at right angles, until he had ridden a long circle. Eventually the trail dropped down into timber; near sundown he came to a spring near which were the dead embers of a campfire.

They stayed here last night, Tune reflected, and made camp.

There wasn't much food left in his saddlebags. He ate sparingly, and estimating the distance to Indian Joe Spears' store, reckoned it was a good fifteen or twenty miles northeast of him.

He lay awake for hours, his mind tromping a treadmill of nagging questions, and seeking answers. Why had the rustlers split up his herd? What were they up to, and how far ahead were they? He thought about Jim Beam, hiding out in these same hills, and about Tracey Fayette who was wearing Jim's ring.

The sun was nine o'clock high when Tune awoke the next morning. As he was saddling his pony, five Big T cows straggled in single file to the spring. Presently circling through a stand of stunted pine, he found a dozen more of his cows. He was scouting a boulder-studded canyon when a rifle's sharp report shattered the morning silence. That blast of sound was instantly followed by a grunt from his bay pony. The animal lunged and collapsed as Tune rolled headlong from saddle.

Tune's shoulder struck the base of a rock reef, and the horse slid so close that one of its hoofs struck him a glancing blow on the temple. Momentarily dazed, Tune was aware of continuous firing, and the *whang* of bullets ricocheting off rock.

Tune drew up his legs and listened, and decided there were three guns being fired.

Three guns!

He thought instantly, *So they doubled back.* They had set this trap, baiting it with cow tracks.

Only the headlong fall from his dying pony had saved him. Now, reaching over and drawing his Winchester from saddle scabbard, Tune understood that they had him cornered—that they were spread out on three sides of him.

Squinting against the sun, he located one of the guns by its muzzle smoke, slightly above him in a cluster of rocks. He triggered a shot that way, then swiveled around to seek out the other guns.

Presently he saw a man's hat exposed momentarily as that rustler fired. Tune sent an answering shot.

These, he thought, were the men who had killed Juanita. And Manuel. And Pancho. "The dirty bastards," he muttered, and kept watching, hoping for a fair target on which to vent his pent-up hatred.

Two of the guns set up a continuous volley, which puzzled him until he thought, *Covering up for something.* Ignoring those guns, he scanned the canyon to the west and saw a skulking shape move from one boulder to another, so close that he glimpsed this man's face and identified it: Breed Gault, a Spade rider.

All this in the split second it took Tune to squeeze off a shot. Gault lunged to one side, as if hit; he fell behind a boulder and Tune had no target. Quite sure that he had hit Breed, Tune felt a high sense of satisfaction, and thought, *One less gun against me.*

The other two guns were silent now, and Tune guessed they were reloading. Then Gault's gun began blasting, its slug chipping rock fragments from the reef. After that, for a time, while the sun climbed high, there was silence.

Tune studied his position, reckoning his chances of standing them off until dark. There might be a possibility of giving them the slip then, but he'd be afoot. The rock reef slanted around so that it protected him from the north and west, while his dead horse formed a partial barricade to the east. But he had no protection on the south. He wondered how soon they would realize that. . . .

Breed and his two companions began firing again, first one and then the other. The wire-twang passage of bullets was a continuous vibration in Tune's ears, and presently he became aware that one rustler had changed position so that slugs were coming at him from the south.

Tune drew himself tight against the reef. What a hell of a way for a man to fight, he thought—cringing like a cornered coyote. The gun to the south was too far off for accurate shooting, but eventually one of those slugs would find him. He recalled what Keno Smith had told Frank Paddock—that it was the bullets you don't hear that do the damage. He wondered how Keno was, and if they would ever share a bottle of bourbon again.

Tune fired at Gault, who was nearest him, and saw his bullet bounce harmlessly off rock. When he turned to look for muzzle smoke to the east, he discovered that this rustler had moved closer—was within twenty five yards of him.

Closing in, Tune thought, reloading his gun. When he counted the remaining cartridges in his belt, he found only eleven.

In that moment Lew Tune realized he was doomed. The though came to him that the same cattle that had cost Juanita, Manuel and Pancho their lives would cost him his.

Ambition, he reflected morosely.

Oddly, then, he understood that Jim Beam had been caught in the same trap—and for the same reason. Jim had been ambitious also, because he wanted to marry Tracey Fayette.

He glimpsed the man on the south, skulking toward a windfall, fired at him and missed. Tune knew then it was just a matter of time before they took him.

CHAPTER **8**

CONSERVING his cartridges, Tune crouched and watched, and waited for the final play. He might, he thought, kill one of them when they rushed him. If he were lucky, he

to him that he didn't know the man's name, but it made no difference. He was nothing now. Tune felt no pity for him, nor any hatred.

Isham squatted on his heels and scooped up a handful of dirt, feeling it with his thumb as it sifted from his fingers. Watching this, Tune wondered about him. He had seen dry farmers feel the texture of earth; it was an habitual thing with them. But it seemed odd for a cattleman.

"How about it?" Melotte asked impatiently. "You riding for Anchor or not?"

Isham glanced sourly at his straw boss, said, "Not your business, Whitey."

Melotte accepted the reprimand without apparent resentment; he was, Tune thought, wholly obedient to Isham's wishes.

For a little interval no one spoke. Then Tune said, "There's two things that need to be settled first. Jim Beam is my friend. I'll help him any way I can."

"That's all right, within reason," Isham agreed. "What's the other thing?"

"I've got to gather my cattle and put them on Beam's place."

"We'll help you," Isham said.

Tune took a deep drag on his cigarette and exhaled the smoke with a sigh. "All right, Tilt. I'll ride for Anchor."

"Good," Isham said. Turning to Brite and Clawson, he ordered, "Go find these two jiggers' ponies. Turn one loose, and Lew will ride the other."

As the punchers rode off, Tune asked, "You know these dead ones?"

"I know their names—Taber and Bascom. A couple of the renegade bunch Cameron has hired to fight Anchor. White trash. And he's got upwards of twenty of them."

"How many men on your payroll?" Tune asked.

"Well, there's six of us working up here, four line-camp men riding patrol, and a hay crew on Big Meadow. Fifteen counting you."

Tune glanced at the dead man again. He said, "Two more to go—Breed Gault and Bart Hayden."

"Hayden?" Melotte asked. "Why him?"

"You hear what happened on the Reservation Road?"

Whitey nodded.

"Hayden is the bastard behind that raid," Tune muttered. "He hired these men to jump my herd."

47

Isham smiled, showing a flash of his old joviality. "This makes it just dandy, Lew. I hear Hayden has thrown in with Cameron to fight Anchor, so you've joined the right outfit."

Later, when Tune was transferring his saddle to the Spade horse, Brite asked, "How about the dead men?"

"Gault knows where they are," Isham said. "If Cameron wants their corpses, he can come and get them."

The five riders began rounding up Tune's cattle, working until midafternoon and then driving the gather to Sand Creek, where Anchor's chuck wagon was stationed.

Two riders drifted in just before dark, driving a small bunch of Anchor stock to the holding ground.

Tune ate a bounteous supper that night. Later, sitting at the fire and listening to the talk around him, he thought; *So now I'm an Anchor rider.*

Breed Gault had punished his pony leaving the canyon. He had seen his companions fall, and had only one thought —to get away. Those Anchor guns were too reachy.

Later in the afternoon he rode his sweat-lathered horse up to a Spade line camp. There was no one in the shack, but three spare horses drowsed in a corral. Hastily transferring his saddle to a fresh mount, Breed rode away from the camp at a lope.

Near sundown he began angling out of the hills, reaching the flats south of Spade shortly after dark. It was past nine o'clock when he rode into headquarters, stopping his spent pony in front of the main house.

A shaft of doorway lamplight revealed Riley Cameron and Bart Hayden standing on the veranda.

Cameron called at once, "Who is it?"

"Me—Breed," Gault announced. "All hell has broke loose!"

Men were coming up from the bunkhouse now, and Cameron demanded, "What do you mean?"

"Anchor shot us up. Bascom and Taber got it. I don't know how bad."

The crew, shadowy shapes in the yard, had gathered around Gault. Hayden said sharply, "Don't sit out there and shout—come inside."

Breed resented that. His swarthy, sweat-greased face rutted into a scowl; in the lamplight his features appeared wholly mongoloid.

"Come on in," Cameron said, his voice smoothly inviting. "You need a drink."

Following Gault and Cameron into the house, Hayden closed the door. "I don't want that bunch knowing all my business," he muttered.

Cameron poured Gault a drink. He asked, "What happened?"

"Well, we had Tune dead to rights, in that canyon just north of Pine Top Spring," Breed said. He gulped down the drink, adding, "I ain't had nothing to eat since breakfast."

Cameron, a lathy, dark-faced man with an enormous nose and frosty blue eyes, said, "The cook will fix you something. You say you had Tune cornered?"

Breed nodded, and held out his glass for a refill. "We were closing in on him when Anchor jumped us from up above—five or six guns. Maybe more."

"You think Bascom and Taber were killed?" Cameron asked.

"They must've been. We had no protection from them high guns. I never ducked so much lead in my life. It was pure luck that I got away."

Hayden asked impatiently, "Where are my forty head of steers?"

"We started them across the malpais," Breed said. "They should be down around Willow Spring by now."

An acquisitive glint brightened Breed's sooty eyes as he said, "If Bascom and Taber are dead, you can pay me their share. By God, I earned it."

"I want to see my steers before I pay anything," Hayden said.

Ignoring this exchange, Cameron reflected, "Isham has been spoiling for a fight. Now, by God, we'll give him a war."

CHAPTER 9

IT took one more day to gather the rest of Tune's cattle— a hundred and forty-eight head. The next day Tune, Isham and two Anchor hands moved the Big T herd to Beam's place on the northern slope of the hills.

Tune and Isham were riding together toward Beam's shack when Anchor's boss said, "You're lucky they didn't scatter your stuff more."

That made Tune remember the tracks going toward the malpais. He halted his horse and said gustily, "By God, we didn't find them all. Keno's forty head of steers are missing."

He told Isham about the pool steers, and Hayden's attempt to welch on the deal.

"By now they've been mixed with Hayden's stuff," Isham predicted.

"I've got to get them," Tune said. "I won't see Keno cheated."

Isham said, "There's only one way you can collect those steers."

"How's that?"

"If Anchor smashes Spade—puts that damned spread out of business once and for all," Isham said. He thought about this for a moment, then added, "So you've got a stake in this fight, friend Lew. Keno Smith's forty steers."

They rode on, and soon came to Beam's shack. Tune opened the door and gave the room a quick appraisal. It was, he saw, a typical bachelor layout—the unmade bed, the table with its clutter of staples in their store containers, the unwashed skillet on the stove.

He turned to Isham, who had remained asaddle, and asked, "Want a cup of coffee?"

Isham shook his head. "Got to get back to the roundup. I'll have the cook leave you some provisions when he goes by here tomorrow."

"I'd like to go into town within the next day or so," Tune said, "to see Keno."

"If Keno comes out of it all right, tell him I'm hiring men," Isham suggested. His face was grave when he added, "Cameron has me outnumbered. There's been an influx of scum around these parts since Sheriff Slaughter ran the horsethieves out of Cochise County. They've hired out at Spade, or are riding grubline there."

"You think Cameron will start something right away?"

"I'll be surprised if he doesn't, now that we've killed two of his men. Your patrol is from here to the Lost Horse line camp. Keep your eyes peeled for tracks through the pass, and down on Apache Flats. That's Spade's shortest route to Anchor."

Isham was on the point of leaving when Tune said flatly,

"I've got to tell you this, just to keep the record straight. I'm convinced that Melotte jobbed Jim Beam."

Isham's craggy face remained impassive, but his brown eyes narrowed, placing a sharp scrutiny on Tune as he said, "I choose to think otherwise. Whitey has his faults. He's a trifle brash, and he talks too much. But I don't think he'd deliberately job a man."

He rode out of the yard then, sitting tall and proud in the saddle. Watching him disappear into the yonder brush, Tune thought, *I was right about him*. If Beam had been framed, Isham hadn't ordered it.

He led his horse to the corral and unsaddled. Surveying the lean-to shed and a rickety wagon with a wire-mended tongue, Tune saw that the place hadn't changed any in the past two years. It was still a cow camp, nothing more.

Afterward, Tune busied himself cleaning up the shack. Jim, he reflected, was a slovenly housekeeper. He tried to picture Tracey Fayette in this place, and could not. She was a town girl, used to the conveniences of town living. Toting water from the windmill well, he thought, *This isn't for Tracey*.

He was chopping wood when Indian Joe Spears drove into the yard in a buckboard loaded with provisions for his Hoodoo Hills store.

"I was going past and heard you chopping wood," the fat trader said. "Wondered who was here."

It occurred to Tune that Spears would know where Beam was hiding out. He asked, "Seen Jim lately?"

Indian Joe's beady eyes glanced about the place, as if fearful someone might hear his reply. Then he said, "Jim came into my store a couple of nights ago."

"When you see him again tell Jim I'm here," Tune said. "You been to Reservation?" The lardy trader nodded. "How's Keno Smith?"

"Well, he's alive."

Spears drove on out to the trail then, the crooked wheels of his ancient rig monotously squeaking for lack of grease.

After supper, Tune toted his blankets out into the brush and bedded down. The shack's warped pine boards wouldn't stop bullets, he reasoned, and one of these nights Spade would come calling.

He rode patrol the next day, coming to the Lost Horse line camp shortly before noon. The man stationed here was out riding patrol, but there was coffee in the pot, bread and beef for a sandwich. The log cabin, built into the side of a hill which formed its rear wall, was neat and clean. There were two shirts, a suit of underwear and three pairs of socks drying on a clothesline. Tune wondered about the puncher who lived here alone, and fashioned a mental picture of a man past middle age, fastidious and a bit on the cranky side.

Riding back across Apache Flats, Tune glimpsed a dust plume far to the west. That would be on Spade range, some eight or ten miles away. He dismounted and smoked a cigarette, watching the smear of dust slowly inch toward the northwest. Those riders, he thought, would come onto Anchor range up around Red Mesa, which was on the other man's patrol beat.

So thinking, Tune rode into the hills, reaching Beam's shack at sundown.

After feeding his horse, he cooked supper and ate it. This, he reflected, was a lonely life.

A remote sound, like that of a walking horse, caused Tune to blow out the lamp. For a moment then, he stood unmoving, trying to pick up the sound again—wondering if Spade riders were out there in the moonless dark. There was no sound now. Stepping to the doorway, he listened again, keening the night air for fully five minutes without hearing anything.

Might have been a cow, he thought. Going outside, he circled the shack, stopping frequently to listen.

Satisfied at last, Tune went inside and lighted the lamp. He was washing the supper dishes when Jim Beam said, "Hello, Lew."

Tune whirled, reaching for his gun. He said angrily, "Don't sneak up on a man." Then he grinned and invited, "Come into your parlor, Jim."

Beam's round, whisker-shagged face was tight with apprehension. He glanced over his shoulder, and said fretfully, "They might trap me in here."

"Don't think they're looking for you," Tune said.

But Beam faded from the doorway; he was standing in the deep shadows when Tune went out and shook hands with him.

"I circled the place twice before I came in," Beam said. "No telling when Anchor will come snooping. Let's get away from the shack."

They crossed the dark yard to the corral where Beam had left his horse. He asked, "Did Tracey tell you about her and me?"

52

"Yes, and congratulations," Tune said, forcing an enthusiasm he didn't feel. Then he added, "I never thought you'd make it."

"We aren't married yet. The way things are going maybe we never will be. This is a hell of a deal, Jim—being on the dodge. It gets a man down."

"Maybe you should quit dodging and stand trial," Tune suggested.

"With Anchor against me? I wouldn't stand a chance."

He was, Tune thought, as pessimistic as a man should be. Jim had never been exactly jovial, except when he was drinking. But he had always been hopeful, and appeared to be convinced that hard work combined with frugality would pay off for him someday.

Beam abruptly clutched Tune's arm, whispered, "Listen!"

Tune didn't hear anything; he thought, *You're spooky*, and was on the verge of speaking, when the rumor of walking horses came to him. He said, "Stay still," and went quickly to the shack.

Blowing out the lamp again, he hurried outside and waited near the rear wall while the tromp of horses coming into the yard was a steadily increasing sound against the night's stillness.

"All right, Tune—you can light the lamp," a voice called casually.

"Whitey?" Tune asked.

"Yes, I brought you a couple of horses."

Tune had the lamp lighted when Melotte drew up before the shack with two led horses. Tune took the lead ropes and invited, "Have some coffee?"

"Don't mind if I do."

"Go in and help yourself," Tune suggested, "while I corral these ponies."

Beam was asaddle, poised for flight when Tune passed close to him and whispered, "Stay still," and went on to the corral gate. When he was back to the shack, Melotte was drinking coffee and smoking a cigarette.

"How's the roundup going?" Tune inquired.

"We'll wind up this end of it tomorrow. Seen any Spade riders?"

Tune shook his head. "Saw dust over to the west today. Looked like they might be heading toward Red Mesa."

Then, looking Melotte in the eye, Tune asked, "Why did you frame Jim Beam?"

The unexpectedness of the question threw Melotte off

balance. His normally hooded eyes popped wide for a moment, flashing tawny in the lamplight, and he demanded, "Who says I framed him?"

"I do," Tune said. "I'm sure of it."

Melotte contemplated him with squinting intensity for a moment before saying, "So, what if I did. You'd have a hell of a time proving it."

"Maybe not," Tune said, very deliberate about this. "If Jim stands trial, it won't look good for you—especially the part about Tracey Fayette."

"Keep her out of it!" Melotte commanded, a ruddy flush staining his clean-shaven cheeks. He stood up, as if suddenly eager to leave. He said, "She's got nothing to do with it."

"But a jury might think different, Whitey. They might think it odd that the cow hide was discovered by you so soon after Tracey accepted Jim's ring."

Tune had been guessing, not sure about the time element, but knew instantly he had hit home. Completely flustered now, Melotte said, "You pull Tracey into this and I'll kill you!"

Tune laughed at him. He said, "Two can play that game, Whitey. Thanks for warning me."

Melotte went out to his horse. Mounting, he said, "Keep your long nose out of my business, Tune," and went charging out of the yard.

Presently, when he was quite sure Melotte had kept going, Tune went back to the corral.

"What did I tell you?" Beam said. "By God, that was a close one."

"Calm down," Tune urged. "You're strung tight as a wire."

Beam said irritably, "You would be, too, if you was on the dodge."

"I'm going into town tomorrow, to see how Keno Smith is," Tune said. "It'll be about dark when I get there."

"So?" Beam asked.

"If you want to come along I'll meet you at Spanish Fork about noon. You won't need to be seen. I'll go into the Acme and tell Tracey you're out back."

"I'd sure like to see her," Beam said. "It's hell to have a girl like Tracey and not be able to see her."

"You could talk it over—about giving yourself up," Tune suggested.

Beam thought about it for a long moment. Then he said,

"I'll ride in with you, Lew. Anything is better than this waiting and dodging. By God, I'm going loco. That's a fact. Always looking over my shoulder. Sneaking into Indian Joe's store at night. If it wasn't for Tracey I'd leave the country."

That frank outburst of futility told Tune that this man, who had appeared so self-sufficient, was feeling genuinely sorry for himself. Jim, Tune thought, wasn't quite as much of a man as he had seemed to be. Yet this realization didn't alter Tune's sense of friendship. He merely felt sorry for him.

"I'll meet you at noon," Beam said, and rode off, cautiously keeping his horse at a walk.

Shortly after dark that night three Spade riders had swooped down on the Lost Horse line camp, shooting at the cabin's lamplit window while another rider hazed two horses from the corral.

The Anchor man hastily blew out the lamp, his face tilted above the globe; the lamp went out at the precise instant a bullet bored through his forehead.

The raiders swept on, driving two Anchor horses ahead of them.

Afterward one of the Spade men said, "Jack Medwick is afoot, and don't know it."

At about this same hour Breed Gault and three companions raided Anchor's roundup camp in the Hoodoos. But Tilt Isham, expecting trouble, had prepared a welcome for them.

Four sacks of grain, covered with blankets, reposed near the campfire's glowing coals. In that faint illumination the sacks looked like sleeping men. But the crew, bedded down far beyond the circle of firelight, made no targets—until their guns began blasting at the four raiders who charged through camp.

A Spade rider croaked a curse, and fell into the embers, and lay there unmoving as his clothing caught fire. A horse went down, turning a complete somersault, and landed on its rider with a crushing impact.

When the raid was over, four sacks of grain were riddled with bullets and the cook's coffeepot was punctured.

A quarter of a mile beyond the roundup camp, Breed Gault pulled up his mount. He yelled, "Over here," and waited for his companions to join him.

55

One man angled in through the pines.

"Those Anchor bastards must of knowed we was coming," Breed muttered. "But we sure got those near the fire."

Then he asked impatiently, "Where's Freddie and Bill?"

"They went down," his companions said. "You sure them shapes by the fire was men?"

It had occurred to Breed that Isham might have tricked him into an ambush trap. But now he said, "Of course I'm sure. One of 'em was reaching for a gun when I shot him."

Presently, as they rode through the night's quilted gloom, Breed said, "I'm telling Riley we killed four Anchor men. Don't you say no different."

CHAPTER 10

FRESHLY shaved and wearing a clean shirt, Tune started for Reservation soon after sunup. There was no hurry and so he dawdled along the trail, replenishing his memories of these hills. He passed two nester shacks where women and their broods of children gawked at him, and shortly after ten o'clock came to the little settlement called Tailholt, where Indian Joe Spears' store was the only business establishment.

Tune stopped in front of the log building that was a combination store and saloon, exchanging brief greetings with two men who were sunning themselves on the stoop. When he went inside, Indian Joe asked, "You hear the news?"

Tune shook his head, whereupon Spears said, "Spade raided Anchor's roundup camp last night and lost two men."

"How about Anchor?"

"Nobody got hit. I guess Tilt Isham expected the raid and was ready for it. There'll be hell to pay now. Riley Cameron has lost four men this week."

Tune ordered a cup of coffee. He asked slyly, "Whose side are you on, Joe?"

"Neither one, by God. I'm a businessman—can't afford to take sides. Whose side are you on?"

"Well, I'm working for Anchor," Tune said. "I'm on the payroll."

That admission obviously surprised Indian Joe. As if attempting to get this straight, he said, "You're staying at Jim Beam's place, and working for Isham who is hunting for Jim. It don't add up."

Amused at his puzzlement, Tune offered no explanation. He finished his coffee and went out to his horse.

Indian Joe came to the doorway. He said, "I told Jim you was over there."

"Thanks," Tune said, and rode off.

News of his employment, he thought, would spread through these hills as rapidly as the report of last night's fight had traveled. . . .

When Tune came to Spanish Fork, Beam was waiting. Seeing Jim in daylight now, Tune observed what being on the dodge had done to this man who had been so self-contained. Jim's eyes held the harassed, almost frantic expression of a hunted thing, and his beard-blurred features were tightly drawn. He wasn't self-contained now; he was as wary and nervous as a cornered coyotte.

Beam asked, "See any Anchor riders?"

Tune shook his head. "They're all over in the roughs, working cattle. You've nothing to worry about today."

As they rode through a stand of tall pines, Beam said, "This country used to look good to me. It don't any more. I'd like to sell out and take Tracey to some other place." He thought about it for a moment before adding, "Maybe I'll have a talk with Riley Cameron. He offered me a thousand dollars last year."

"I'd give you more than that," Tune said.

"You got that much cash?"

"I will have, soon as I sell some steers. But I think you can keep your place if you'll stand trial."

They rode out of the hills late in the afternoon. Here the trail angled into the road to Anchor; observing three sets of fresh horse tracks going north, Beam said at once, "Anchor riders been in town today. I don't feel safe in this open country. No telling when we'll run into somebody—Sheriff Dixon, maybe."

"Soon be dark," Tune suggested.

Tilt Isham had arrived in Reservation shortly before noon, inquiring for Dixon and being told the sheriff was out of town. During the afternoon Isham had hired three men as hay hands, and sent them out to Anchor. He also had a long talk with the president of the Reservation Bank, discussing Anchor's credit and the possibility of stretching it a little in case there was a long-drawn-out fight with Spade.

Isham was sitting on the Palace Hotel veranda with Jake Steinheimer when Sheriff Dixon rode into town at dusk. Ten minutes later Isham sat in the jail office, telling Dixon about last night's raid.

"The preliminaries are over," he said. "From now on it's war—and we might as well face it."

"We?" Dixon asked.

Isham nodded. "You can't stay neutral in this one, Jeff. You've got to decide which side you're going to back. If you pick the wrong side, you'll be out of a job when it's over."

Dixon, who had been a politician most of his adult life, didn't like that blunt declaration. Always before he had managed to maintain a strict neutrality and the appearance, at least, of being his own man. It was in his nature to follow a pattern that had proved successful and so he demanded, "Why is this any different than the last time Anchor tangled with Spade? I didn't interfere then—why should I interfere now?"

"Because this one is final. It's my guess there'll be no Spade when it's over. Either that or there'll be no Anchor. The shooting has already started. I'm expecting a raid on Anchor headquarters any time. I hired three men this afternoon to cut hay so I can pull in three cowboys to guard Anchor. But I'll need those riders to operate with the rest of my crew."

"What do you want me to do?" Dixon asked.

"Send your two deputies out to guard my headquarters," Isham said.

Dixon stared at him. "I can't do that," he exclaimed. "You can't expect me to go that far. What would Riley Cameron say?"

Isham made a chopping motion with his right hand. He said harshly, "To hell with what Cameron says. Anchor pays big taxes in this county. I've got a right to ask for protection of my property. That's all your deputies would be doing—protecting property against unlawful trespass."

Dixon's voice revealed his dislike for the proposal as he inquired, "Suppose Cameron asked me to do the same thing?"

"He hasn't—because he's not bright enough," Isham

insisted. "It's a legal maneuver, Jeff. So legal that Riley wouldn't think of it. I'm within my rights asking for protection, and it's your duty to give it."

"Suppose I refuse?" Dixon asked.

Anchor's boss eyed him sharply for a moment before saying, "You'd be all through as sheriff if Anchor wins—and be goddamn sure that I intend to win."

Dixon thought about that, the contradictory run of his thinking visible on his frowning face. He said, "I haven't got many years left, and I'd like to finish them wearing a badge."

"Exactly," Isham said.

"But supposing Spade wins? Anchor is outnumbered, ain't it?"

Isham nodded.

"Then what makes you think you'll win?"

Isham made the chopping motion again. He said, "Most of my men have been working for Anchor a long time. They're loyal. That scum at Spade will fold up in the clutch. When the final showdown comes, they'll run like rats deserting a sinking ship."

Isham waited out an interval while Dixon accepted the logic of that reasoning. Then he asked, "What's it going to be, Jeff? Do I get those two deputies?"

"All right," Dixon muttered. "I'll send them out in the morning."

Isham smiled, and his voice turned jovial as he said, "You've decided right, Jeff. And you'll be wearing that badge long after Riley Cameron is dead."

At about this same time, Lew Tune stepped into the Acme Restaurant. Tracey Fayette, busy with a customer at the cash register, smiled at him as he took a table. When she came over to him, Tune said quietly, "Jim is out back. He wants to see you."

CHAPTER 11

THE waitress who took Tune's order was a rather striking brunette, and apparently knew it. She smiled at him in a flirty way that reminded him of June Patterson; yet, because Tracey was outside with Jim Beam, Tune couldn't

59

get into the spirit of the thing—couldn't divert his thinking from the reunion that was taking place in the dark
alley.

They'd be in each other's arms, he thought. Tracey and
Jim, kissing one another.

None of my business, he told himself, and watched the
waitress make change for a customer. She wore a peekaboo
blouse that accentuated her breasts; when she walked to
the kitchen he observed the rhythmic sway of her hips. As
she brought him his supper, Tune asked, "You're new here,
aren't you?"

She shook her head. "New to you, maybe, but I've
been here almost a year."

It was an odd thing. She was receptive, and he had an
evening in town. But he felt no real interest in her. All he
could think of was Tracey. Tracey in Jim Beam's arms.
Tracey kissing, and being kissed . . .

When he paid his bill the waitress smiled at him again,
and Tune thought, *I must be getting old*. Walking to the
hotel through the dark street, he wondered if Tracey would
convince Jim he should give himself up and stand trial.

As he stepped up to the Palace veranda, Frank Paddock
rose from a chair and said, "Lew—I'm glad to see you."

As they shook hands, Paddock said, "I'd like to talk to
you—ask your advice."

"Can it wait until I go up and see how Keno is?"

"Sure, and Keno is doing fine. I saw him an hour ago."

Tune went upstairs and found Smith on the bed, dressed
in his pants and undershirt.

"It's about time you showed up," Smith greeted.

He appeared pale, and there was a freshly healed scar on
his head, but his grip was like a vise when Tune shook his
hand and asked, "How you feeling?"

"Puny," Smith said. "Puny as a poisoned pup."

Presently, when Smith had his pipe going, he said, "I'm
a trifle ashamed of the way those sonsabitches got the jump
on us, Lew. But we wasn't expecting nothing like that.
One of them said something to Manuel—I couldn't hear
what he said. Manuel started to draw his gun, and then all
three of 'em was shooting at us. Just like that. We didn't
have a chance."

"Well, two of the bastards are dead," Tune said. "I'll get
the other two, in time."

"Two?"

"Including Bart Hayden. He hired those three."

Smith said, "I figured it was his doings. On account of my forty steers."

"We'll get the steers back, Keno. It may take some time, but we'll get them."

They visited for a time, Tune telling him about his narrow escape from the killers and how he had paid for that rescue by joining Anchor's fight against Spade.

"Tell Tilt Isham I'll be out to give him a hand, soon as I get loose of this sawbones," Keno said.

Later, when Tune went down to the veranda, Frank Paddock said, "My shoulder was bothering me bad, so I came in to see the doctor. He had to open it up."

Tune asked, "What do you think of that Spade outfit?"

"Well, they've got some tough characters out there, Lew. And they's fixing for a big fight, according to the talk."

"Where does that leave you?" Tune asked.

Paddock shrugged. "Tate and I wanted to pull out of the combine, but Bart wouldn't hear of it. He used our pool cattle to buy an interest in Spade."

"Thought so," Tune mused. Presently he said, "This fight is going to get rough, Frank—awful rough. You and Tate and the boy don't belong in it. Pull out, even if you have to leave your cattle."

Paddock said dejectedly, "We'd hate to lose our cattle, after five years of hard work."

"Maybe you wouldn't lose them—if Anchor wins," Tune said. "You could show ownership, and make a legal claim—if you don't take part in the fight."

"And you think Anchor would give us our cattle afterward?"

"Tilt Isham is a fair man. He doesn't want your cattle. His fight is against Riley Cameron."

Paddock absorbed that information in silence. Finally he said, "I sure don't want to fight. And neither does Tate. It's all Bart's idea."

"You listen to Hayden, you'll get yourself killed," Tune said. "Think it over."

Then he walked back to the restaurant.

The Acme was closed for the night. Tune walked on past it and stood in the deeper darkness under the barbershop's wooden awning. There wasn't much traffic on Main Street. He wondered if Jim and Tracey were through visiting out back. . . .

Presently a pair of men walked along the street from the direction of Fancy Mayme's parlorhouse. One of them complained, "That little bitch always tries to take my last dollar."

Then Tune saw two men come out of Faro Charlie's Saloon. In the bloom of doorway lamplight he identified Tilt Isham and Sheriff Jeff Dixon. He watched these two walk toward Pelky's Livery and had his amused thought that this was probably the closest Jim Beam and Tilt Isham had been to each other since Jim had gone on the dodge.

Tune went on to the alley and turned into its long lane of pitch darkness, and heard Isham ride past the alleyhead on his way out of town. Tilt, he thought, would probably go to Anchor headquarters tonight.

Tune passed the horses he and Beam had left tied to a fence in the alley. Beyond them a faint shaft of lamplight came from the restaurant's rear window. The back door was closed, but now, as he approached, Tracey Fayette called expectantly: "Lew?"

She was at the dark end of the stoop, and Tune thought, *Standing guard for Jim.*

Tune said, "Yes." He found her vague shape in the shadows, and felt stirred as he always did at her presence. The scent of her perfume was a remembered delicacy; without thinking, Tune reached out for her and in this moment they were as they had formerly been.

"No, Lew," she protested as he tried to kiss her.

Then the door opened and Jim Beam stood there, asking fretfully, "Who is it?"

Tracey turned to him at once, saying, "Lew is here," and Tune followed her inside.

Beam had been eating at the kitchen table. He sat down again, saying, "This is the first good meal I've had in a week."

Tune took a chair, and Tracey asked, "Want something to eat?"

"Just coffee," Tune said, and couldn't keep his eyes off her. She was, he thought, everything a man wanted in a woman. He had known this before, two years ago. But he hadn't asked her to marry him, and now it was too late.

Tracey brought him a cup of coffee and then took a chair at the table. The bracket lamp was turned low; its faint illumination, like candlelight, gave her face a shadowed loveliness that strongly pulled at Tune's attention, and he thought, *What a woman!*

He was remotely aware of resentment toward Beam,

which seemed odd until he realized this was the old story of triangle—of two men wanting the same woman. Tune felt guilty then; he asked, "How does it seem to be back in town, Jim?"

"Good, mostly, but I don't like having to sneak around. It's spooky."

He was, Tune thought, a thoroughly cautious man. Jim didn't like to take chances. He wanted security, and the orderly way of living that went with industriousness and frugality. To that extent, at least, Jim would make a good married man.

Tracey looked at Beam and then at Tune, unconsciously comparing them, thinking how unlike they were in so many ways. It seemed odd that they should be friends. And she felt a sense of shame at the unruly emotions Tune had stirred in her. He was never quite the same; there seemed always to be a different facet of his personality for discovery. Remembering how upset and remorseful he had been about the Mexican girl's death, she thought, *He has accepted it.*

The same as he had accepted her being engaged to Jim Beam.

She was aware of Tune's continuing appraisal, and now he asked, "What do you think, Tracey? Hadn't he better turn himself in and stand trial?"

"I don't know," she said, making a small gesture of futility with her hands. "A jury probably wouldn't find him guilty, but it might."

Beam said, "I'd rather sell out and leave—if you'd go with me."

"Where would we go?" Tracey asked, revealing her dislike for his proposal in the way she added, "Besides, I've got a good business here."

For a moment all three of them were silent, thinking about it. Finally Tune said, "You're no thief, Jim. They've got to prove you are before they send you to the pen. Whitey Melotte will sound silly, testifying against you. It's well known he had a case on Tracey. He doesn't want you to stand trial. He knows how flimsy the evidence is against you. If the jury found you innocent, it would prove that he framed you on account of Tracey."

"But I never gave him any encouragement," Tracey insisted.

Her indignation amused Tune. He asked, "You never smiled at him?"

"Well, yes, but—"

"That's all the encouragement any man would need," Tune said, a self-mocking smile slanting his cheeks.

Tracey looked at him in the perplexed fashion of a woman not sure whether she was being complimented or insulted. "Perhaps Lew is right," she said thoughtfully. "You can't go on this way, Jim. And you shouldn't leave the country."

"But it would mean going to jail until my trial comes up, and that might be weeks—months even," Beam muttered.

"No—if they won't accept your place for bail, I'll put up a cash bond," Tracey assured him. "Then you could stay in town until your trial."

Watching Beam now, Tune thought Jim's face held the expression of a boy listening to his mother as he asked, "Are you sure that's the right thing to do?"

And in this moment, remembering how Tracey had said, "*Poor Jim,*" Tune understood why Tracey had accepted Beam's ring—she felt sorry for him. Not just that, of course; she had liked him a lot, Jim was a personable fellow and handsome in clean-cut, mannish way. But her feeling sorry for him had tipped the scales in Jim's favor. He appealed to some protective instinct in her.

Tracey glanced at Tune, asking for confirmation; when he nodded, she said, "Yes, Jim. I think it's the best thing to do."

Beam loosed a gusty sigh. He said, "I hope you're right." Then he added nervously, "Let's get it done," and got up at once.

Ten minutes later Tune found Sheriff Dixon in the saloon. He said, "Jim Beam is over at your office. Wants to give himself up."

"The hell you say!" Dixon exclaimed. He gulped down the remainder of his drink, and reflected, "Whitey Melotte won't like this at all. He asked me not to look for Beam."

That admission angered Tune. "You knew it was a frame-up and you did nothing about it," he accused.

"No, I didn't have any reason to think that," Dixon defended. "Whitey just said it would be simpler if Beam left the country. A rustling charge is hard to prove, sometimes."

"This one will be," Tune said. "It'll prove just one thing —that Melotte jobbed Beam."

Dixon shrugged and turned wearily away from the bar. "Trouble, trouble," he muttered. "And it's going to get worse. Being sheriff of this county ain't my idea of a cinch."

"Judge Ross in town?" Tune asked.

Dixon shook his head. "Won't be back for a couple of weeks."

"What is the customary bail?"

"Five hundred dollars."

"Jim's place should be sufficient for that," Tune suggested.

"Maybe the county attorney won't accept it, the way things are," Dixon said. "He might want a cash bond."

"Tracey is with Jim. She'll put up the cash if you insist," Tune said.

When Dixon left, Faro Charlie said, "You talk Beam into giving himself up?"

"I recommended it, but Tracey convinced him."

The saloonman eyed him wonderingly, said, "It would have been better for you if Beam had quit the country."

"How so?"

"You got a case on Tracey, ain't you?" Charlie asked. "It sure beats hell how a good woman can mix things up, if she's a looker. Whitey Melotte, Jim Beam and you. All skirt-crazy."

Tune paid for his drink. He gave Charlie an appraising consideration, estimating his age at about fifty. "It doesn't seem possible, but you must have been young once yourself," he said, and went out to his horse.

CHAPTER **12**

THERE was a smell of rain in the air when Tune left town shortly before ten o'clock—a pungent odor of wet greasewood and moist adobe earth that told him it was already raining out on the flats west of town. By the time he rode up the first long grade into the Hoodoo Hills it began to drizzle. He unlashed his slicker and got into it, and thought, *This won't make patrol riding a pleasant chore.* There would be no distant dust spirals to signal the approach of Spade riders.

A rising wind whipped the rain into slanting sheets. The night's mealy darkness, combined with a muddy trail, made it necessary for his horse to proceed at a plodding walk. The rain and the gloomy night had a depressing effect on

Tune; he thought, *Nothing has gone right since I came back.* He dredged up the massacre of his three Mexican friends, and cursed morosely. And now, instead of settling the score directly with Hayden, he was involved in a range war.

His pony stopped, as if unsure of the trail ahead. For a moment, as Tune peered into the darkness, he could think of no reason for his mount's behavior; then it occurred to him that they were probably at Spanish Fork and the pony didn't know which trail to take. Lighting a match, he shielded it with his hand long enough to confirm his guess, and then reined the pony up the west fork. Soon after that a blacker shape loomed against the night's opaque darkness and a voice demanded; "Who's there?"

Tune stopped at once. Reaching inside his slicker, he drew his gun, and heard the yonder rider maneuver his horse off the trail. He was peering into the quilted gloom, not sure of the man's location, when the fellow said irritably, "Speak up—is that you, Baldy?"

The silence built up now, broken only by the dripping branches of high pines. Tune had the advantage, for he had not moved and the yonder rider couldn't exatly locate him. The fellow put his horse in motion again, cautiously circling through the trees off to the right of the trail. Tune was half-turned in saddle, following that sound, when another voice called from behind him, "Where in hell are you at?"

"Look out," the first rider warned. "There's someone betwixt us."

Still not knowing whether they were Spade or Anchor riders, Tune eased his horse forward, wanting to ride out of this. He had barely got started when a gun blasted off to the right of him, the bullet snarling wide by a foot or more. Tune's back muscles flinched as another bullet missed him, yet he kept his pony going and did not return the fire for fear of making a better target.

Both guns opened up behind him now, and he heard the thud of bullets hitting nearby trees. When he had gone a few yards, he turned off the trail and allowed his horse to pick its way through the timber for a short distance before halting again.

The two out there in the trail held a council of war, their voices a remote rumble. Keening the night's dripping darkness, Tune heard their horses pass slowly westward along the trail he had been traveling.

This, he thought, was the way it would be from now on —riders prowling the hills and shooting at any man who failed to identify himself. That was what range war did to a country.

He waited for a full ten minutes or more, wanting to give the pair of riders time to get well ahead of him. Then he rode out to the trail, and followed it, warily alert. The wind had died down, but presently, as he crossed a clearing, Tune noticed that it was rising again. When he got back into timber, the tall pines were steadily sighing.

Tune wondered about the riders ahead of him. This was far to the east of Spade territory, yet it would be like Riley Cameron to maintain far-ranging patrols. Spade's owner had a big crew at his disposal and he was the type of man who would want them to earn their pay.

It was coming daylight when Tune approached the clearing at Tailholt. Halting in the fringe of timber, he gave the obscure settlement a squinting appraisal while rain pelted against his slicker. There was a light at Indian Joe's store, its shine a feeble beacon against the gloomy dawn. He could discern no horses at the hitchrack, but that didn't mean anything; they could have been put in the lean-to barn behind the store.

Deciding to scout the barn, Tune circled slowly through the timber until he was behind a clutter of outbuildings at the rear of the store. The wind had increased so that it made a continuous commotion in the pines; it drove rain across the clearing in slanting sheets that blurred visibility as Tune's pony plodded across a water-sogged field that was fetlock deep in mud. Coming alongside a corral where three horses stood with their tails to the wind, Tune glanced at the rain-fogged outline of the store. There were no lighted windows on this side of the log structure. Unlatching a gate, he rode through it and dismounted under the lean-to's protecting overhang. There were two saddled horses tied to a manger. Tune wasn't sure of their brands until he scrutinized them at close quarters.

So it was Spade, he thought, and resented the bad time they had given him. For a moment, not sure of his next move, Tune considered his choices: he could ride on out, reasonably sure he would see no more of them today— or he could jump them in the store. They were probably eating breakfast.

But there seemed no point in jumping them. Even though they had shot at him, Tune felt no personal animosity toward these two; whoever they were, they had just been doing what was expected of them. Then it occurred to him that one of those Spade riders might be Breed Gault.

That settled it. That gave Tune a compelling motive for plodding across the muddy yard, gun in hand. He was on the point of rounding the store's windowless end when the front door opened. Drawing hastily back, Tune flattened himself against the logs as a man came forward with his head tilted down against the windswept rain; he didn't see Tune until he was within arm's length of him.

Discovery sent him into frantic motion. His right hand snaked inside his slicker; he had his gun half drawn when Tune pistol-whipped him with one savage slash of his gun barrel. The man went down, his hat falling off, and lay still while rain spattered on his bald head. Tune glanced at the stubbled face and thought, *It's not Gault.*

Returning quickly to the barn, Tune took a coiled rope from the saddle of a Spade horse and proceeded to tie the bald one's hands. The fellow grunted, and struggled briefly, like a drunken man.

Tune paid out the rope's coil as he went around to the front door. Standing there for a moment, he heard talk inside, and recognized Indian Joe's high nasal voice. Placing the last few feet of rope around his left arm, Tune opened the door and stepped inside and identified Breed Gault at once.

Breed's eyes bugged wide. He said, "I thought—" and put down his coffee cup. Peering at the leveled gun, he asked, "What's that for?"

Indian Joe sat across the table. He said nervously, "Have some coffee, Lew."

Thinking what Gault had done, Tune felt an almost overwhelming urge to empty his pistol into that startled, mongoloid face. He snarled, "You miserable son of a bitch!"

For an instant he thought Breed would grab his gun. And wished he would, for a wave of hate washed through Tune and the urge to shoot clawed at the brittle thread of his restraint.

Gault sensed this. He put out a hand in an instinctive shielding gesture; he croaked, "No, Tune—no!"

An audible sigh slid from Tune's lips, and now he thought, *I need him alive.* He waggled the gun and said harshly, "Come here."

Gault obeyed at once, keeping his hands chest high as he walked to Tune.

"Turn around," Tune ordered.

He tossed Breed's gun out into the yard, then tied his hands. When he tugged the slack out of the rope he pushed Gault farther into the room until the rope was stretched tight, and said, "Stand there."

Gault asked, "What are you going to do?"

Tune ignored him, and now Indian Joe asked, "Can't we close the door? It's getting cold in here."

"Not yet," Tune said.

He took off his slicker and shaped up a cigarette. Indian Joe brought him a cup of coffee and said, "How about some bacon and eggs?"

"Sure—the eggs straight up."

Abruptly then, the tension ran out of Tune. Afterward, as the good smell of frying bacon came to him, he said, "Nothing like an all-night ride to sharpen a man's appetite."

Observing the slack in the rope now, he walked over to the doorway and saw Gault's partner standing in the rain. "Come in and join the merry throng," he invited.

The man walked in the confused, uncertain way of a drunk; he looked at Gault and said, "You, too?"

Tune closed the door and went back to the table. He said casually, "Spade sure has comical jiggers on its payroll, Joe. Real comical."

The bald rider kept feeling of the discolored lump on his head. He muttered, "Aches like hell," and sat down on a bench.

Breed joined him, his obsidian black eyes watching Tune steadily, like an animal at bay.

Indian Joe dished up the bacon and eggs. He said, "No more trouble in here, Lew. I'm a businessman. It ain't good for me."

"Trouble?" Tune jeered. "What trouble could those two cause now?"

"But this happened in my store, and Riley Cameron won't like it," Spears complained.

Tune shrugged, and ate in the leisurely way of a man relishing his food. Glancing at the bald-headed rider, he asked, "Baldy who?"

"Crouch," the man muttered.

"Sort of a comical name," Tun reflected. "Well, Baldy Crouch, you're in luck. You get to carry the news to Bart Hayden."

"What news?" Gault asked.

"That I've captured the only one of his dirty bastards that's alive," Tune said.

Gault considered that for a moment before asking sullenly, "What are you going to do?"

"I'm going to make you talk—in front of witnesses," Tune said.

It was still raining when he boosted Crouch into his saddle and tied his bound hands to the horn. Leading the horse out of the corral he slapped it on the rump and yelled: "Git!"

Indian Joe stood in the doorway of his store as Tune rode past, leading Gault's horse. Breed's hands were tied to the saddlehorn, his chin tucked into the collar of his slicker.

"There'll be hell to pay," Spears called to Tune.

CHAPTER 13

IT had been well past midnight when Tilt Isham went to bed, but he was up before daylight, eating breakfast with the two men left at Anchor and the three hay hands he had hired in town yesterday.

Fastidious about certain things, Isham was that rarity among cowmen—he shaved every day. His rusty hair, with only a few gray strands showing, was parted precisely in the center, and he was wearing a clean shirt.

A liberal man in most things, Isham would not abide the slightest disloyalty. It was said of him that he had once been enamored of a beautiful girl in Reservation, but had married Anchor instead. There was more truth than jest in that assertion. For twenty-three years, since a drought had burned out his crops on a San Pedro Valley homestead, Isham had worked on this one ranch. Anchor had become a way of life for him—almost an obsession. He had served Mike Cavanaugh, first as a cowpuncher and then as foreman, with an unquestioning faithfulness; now that he was sole proprietor of Anchor, his devotion to the ranch approximated religious fidelity.

Finished with his breakfast, Isham glanced out the kitchen window, observing the wind-slanted rain and saying, "This will play hob with our haying operation."

70

He stoked up the pipe that he smoked only after meals; he said, "It may last for two or three days, Pete. You'd better tote supplies to the line camps before the washes start running full."

"Jack Medwick ordered tea, remember," Pete Maroney said.

"I got it for him yesterday, and a copy of *Harper's Magazine*."

The other regular was Big Joe Walsh, who acted as blacksmith. "An odd one, Medwick," he reflected. "He is for a fact."

"Odd, but strictly loyal to Anchor," Isham said, and gave the three new men a speculative attention. "That's a thing I insist on. Loyalty."

Later, when Maroney had driven off with the tarp-covered supply wagon, Isham said to Walsh, "Take these men out to the hay camp. Bring back Jordan, Kiley and Reeves."

"You expecting trouble from Spade?" Big Joe asked.

"The trouble has already started," Isham said. "They raided our roundup camp night before last."

Then he went to the office and busied himself catching up on his monthly report to the owners in Chicago.

The rain had diminished to a thin drizzle when Lew Tune rode through Anchor's front gate and entered the broad compound bordered by the main house, the bunkhouse, blacksmith shop, commissary, barn and wagon sheds. It was, he thought, exactly as it had been when he worked here, and now he had the same reaction as the first time he had seen it—everything about this place suggested business, and absolute permanence, and power.

He wondered if Breed Gault, sullenly following him on a led horse, had a similar reaction.

Tilt Isham came out to the veranda and stood watching as Tune angled across the compound with Gault.

"Trifle dampish," Tune greeted casually.

It was characteristic of Isham that he merely nodded, and waited for Tune to pull up before saying, "That thing behind you looks exactly like Breed Gault. He's tagging along like you owned him."

"I do," Tune said matter-of-factly. "I wanted to put my mark on him, but it's a bit wet for range branding. Mind if I use your blacksmith shop?"

That took Isham by surprise. He peered at Tune in obvious bewilderment, asked, "The blacksmith shop?"

71

"So I can light up a fire and heat a running iron," Tune explained.

Enlightenment came to Isham then and a thin smile altered his craggy face. "Why, sure," he agreed. "Go right ahead. In fact, I'll help you."

Gault listened to this conversation without a change of expression. He showed nothing beyond a sullen frown as Tune untied him from the saddlehorn and ordered gruffly, "Get down." But later, with a forge fire glowing in the blacksmith shop, Breed asked nervously, "What you fixing to do?"

Tune ignored him. He said to Isham, "Got something I can use for a running iron?"

Isham rummaged around in the shop and presently stuck a rusted iron wagon brace into the fire. He asked, "Where'd you grab this maverick?"

"At Indian Joe's store about daylight this morning," Tune said, and told him the rest of it. Then he added, "Keno said he'd be out to give you a hand, soon as the doctor turns him loose."

It wasn't overly warm in the blacksmith shop, but now perspiration put its shine on Gault's face. He said, "That iron—you trying to spook me into talking?"

Tune had brought his catch-rope into the shop. Now he slipped its noose over Breed's head, took a half-hitch around his boots, and tugged hard on the rope. Gault loosed a choking curse as he went down; he struggled briefly, then as the noose tightened on his throat, he lay perfectly still.

Handing the rope to Isham, Tune proceeded to unbuckle Breed's belt and pull his pants down.

"No—no," Breed gasped. "I'll talk."

Tune put on his right hand glove and picked up the wagon brace. Its end was cherry-red. "You'd better tighten up on the rope, Tilt," Tune suggested. "Don't want to botch this brand."

Afterward, when a T had been burned on Gault's rump and Isham let the rope go slack, Gault wailed, "Goddamn you, Tune!"

As if talking to himself, Tune said softly, "That was for Juanita, Manuel and Pancho." Putting down the iron, he took out his pocket knife and tested its blade on his thumb, and said, "This is for me."

Isham asked wonderingly, "Ear mark?"

Tune nodded, said, "Pull tight on the rope."

All the defiance left Gault now, all the insolence. At

this moment he discarded all pretense of being other than he was—a terror-stricken remnant of a man. "Don't cut me," he gasped pleadingly. "Please don't cut me!"

"So you're afraid of cold steel," Tune mused.

Sweat greased Breed's cheeks and dread dilated his eyes. "I'll talk," he promised. "I'll testify against Hayden."

"In court?" Tune asked.

Breed nodded. He said, "I'm sorry about Keno Smith. He got hit by a stray bullet, I guess."

"How about the others?" Tune demanded. "Those Mexicans were worth a hundred bums like you. By God, I should cut your heart out."

Isham said abruptly, "We've got company," and now, as two men rode up to the shop doorway, he invited, "Get down and rest your saddles."

The slicker-clad deputies came inside, and one of them asked, "What's going on?"

"Teaching a killer to mend his ways," Isham said. Then he turned to Tune and suggested, "If Breed insists on talking, why here's two official witnesses."

Gault recognized the deputies; he said, "Make them turn me loose."

When they just stood there looking at the brand on his rump, Gault whined, "You're peace officers, ain't you? You're supposed to protect citizens."

"This is one of the bastards that raided my herd and killed three people, including a girl," Tune said. "He's no citizen."

Isham said urgently, "This is your last chance, Breed. Are you going to talk?"

Gault glanced at the knife in Tune's hand. He said, "Yes."

"Did you raid Tune's herd?" Isham inquired.

"Yes—Bart Hayden hired us."

"You killed three Mexicans and wounded Keno Smith?" Isham prompted.

"Not just me," Breed said. "Taber and Bascom did some shooting, too."

Isham looked at the deputies, asked, "Is that enough?"

"Enough to charge him with murder," one of them said.

Whitey Melotte and the crew had started the herd of held steers toward Anchor at dawn. When the cattle were headed out, Whitey dropped back in a rear-guard position. It was unlikely that Spade riders would attempt anything in this wind-swept rain, but he was in charge during Isham's absence and the responsibility of protecting the gather was his.

Keeping his pony at a slow jog-trot, Whitey ranged wide on either side of the herd, circling in front of it, and then to the rear. He kept watch for fresh horse tracks in the mud, and would have welcomed sight of them. There was an inherent need for action in Melotte always—an itching desire to impose his will on others. His job as Anchor straw boss fed Whitey's vanity, for it was a position of power in this country second only to that of Tilt Isham.

As the herd neared Tailholt, Whitey discovered fresh horse tracks leading from the settlement and heading off toward the northwest. Instantly suspicious, Melotte drew his gun and followed the tracks for upwards of two miles before circling southward. Finding no fresh tracks here, he loped ahead of the herd; he passed Tailholt, and circling again, discovered that two riders had left the settlement, these traveling toward the northeast.

Wholly aroused now, Melotte doubled back and drew up at Indian Joe's store in a mud-sliding stop. The trader stood in the doorway, and Whitey demanded, "Who was here?"

Spears told him what had occurred. "Tune sent Crouch to Spade and took Gault to Anchor," he concluded. "Now there'll be hell to pay.

The news had a curiously depressing effect on Whitey Melotte. Gault and Crouch, he guessed, had been intending to jump the roundup gather on its way to Anchor. If they had, there would have been a fight—a chance to go into action.

"How long ago did they leave?" he inquired.

"Couple hours ago—just after daylight."

Melotte cursed, and rode back toward the herd. There would be no action today.

Remembering how Tune had upset him the other night by mentioning the possibility that Jim Beam would stand trial and use Tracey Fayette as a witness, Melotte thought angrily, *Him and his long nose!*

Now Tune would make a hit with Isham by his capture of a Spade rider. And besides that, Tune might talk Beam into standing trial, which was a thing Whitey didn't like to think about.

It wouldn't be difficult to eliminate Tune, now that Spade

were horse tracks in the drying mud at the doorway and another set at the east end of the shack. When he went inside, Tune saw that bullets had riddled the bunk's straw tick, the lamp globe had been smashed and a skillet, bottom up on the floor, was punctured. Surveying the damage, Tune thought, *They wouldn't have missed me.* It occurred to him now that this was his third escape from Spade guns —that Lady Luck had her hand on his shoulder. But the law of averages would soon be against him. From here on out it might take more than luck to survive. With that realization nagging at his mind, Tune made a frugal breakfast and ate hurriedly. This shack could be a death trap.

. . .

Tune rode through bright sunshine to the Lost Horse line camp. There were wheel tracks right up to the dugout's door, which seemed odd. The corral gate was open and the extra horses were gone. Nothing inside the camp appeared to be changed, yet there was an air of abandonment about the place. Tune had made himself a sandwich and was eating it when he noticed that the window had been shattered. Contemplating the fragments of glass on the floor, he thought, *Spade has been here.*

Afterwards he stood in the doorway and rolled a cigarette. Glancing at the wheel tracks he wondered why the driver had come up so close. Perhaps he had delivered supplies to the line camp in yesterday's rain. But that didn't explain the open corral gate, nor the broken window.

Tune mounted his horse and was riding out of the yard when it occurred to him that those wheel tracks close to the doorway might mean that a wounded man, or a body, had been removed from the dugout.

There were no fresh tracks crossing his long patrol that day. Nor did he have visitors that night while sleeping out in the brush. But the next day, when he came within sight of the Lost Horse camp, he saw a saddled pony tied to the corral fence and two others inside. Presently, as he rode closer, Tilt Isham came from the dugout.

"Coffee's hot," he announced.

While they ate Isham told about Pete Maroney's discovering old Jack Medwick's body when he came to deliver supplies. "Jack was a good man," Isham said. "He was a tea drinker, but loyal to Anchor. We buried him yesterday. I've got Bob Kiley out here now."

Tune told him about the raid on Beam's shack, and his guess as to why it had been made, whereupon Isham said,

"The steer herd started to town this morning. I'm going in today and I'll swear out a warrant for Hayden's arrest on the basis of Gault's confession."

"You think Dixon will go after him?" Tune asked skeptically.

Isham nodded. "He'll make the ride out to Spade. Probably won't get Hayden, but the warrant will make Hayden a fugitive—which might come in handy if you happened to chop him down."

Tune poured himself another cup of coffee. He said, "Jim Beam gave himself up the other night. He's going to stand trial on Melotte's rustling charge."

"That means Whitey will be tied up in town just when I need him most," Isham said with obvious annoyance.

"Maybe not," Tune suggested. "Maybe Melotte won't testify."

"Why shouldn't he?" Isham inquired.

Tune took a sip of coffee, and then gave the cup a continuing contemplation. He wanted to answer in a way that would drive a wedge of doubt into Isham's mind, and searched for the right words. Finally he said, "Testifying to a damned lie can be a difficult chore. A defense lawyer will want to know how come Melotte found an Anchor hide at Beam's so soon after Tracey Fayette turned Whitey down in favor of Jim."

On the spur of the moment, he added, "And so soon after a beef was slaughtered at Anchor. The lawyer will also want to know why Melotte told Sheriff Dixon not to look for Beam, saying it would be simpler all around if Jim left the country."

"Are you trying to tell me that Beam didn't steal an Anchor beef—that Whitey framed him because of Miss Fayette?" Isham demanded.

Tune nodded.

"I don't believe it," Isham said at once. "Whitey wouldn't use Anchor to perpetrate a personal grudge."

There was something close to arrogance in Isham's manner, as if being employed by Anchor placed a man above suspicion. As if an Anchor man could do no wrong.

"Well, Whitey practically admitted the frame-up to me that night he brought those extra horses," Tune said. "And he threatened to kill me if I talked Tracey into testifying."

Isham peered at him in the prying way of a man of estimating the weight of a steer. His brown eyes took on a penetrating intensity, and he said, "All right. I'll question Whitey about it."

Then, as if eager to end a conversation that disturbed him, Isham got up and went out to his horse. Tune followed him, and as they were parting, Isham said morosely, "The score is one to four in our favor. But Jack Medwick was worth more than all the Spade scum we've killed."

"Counting Breed, Cameron has five less riders than he had a couple weeks ago," Tune pointed out.

"True," Isham agreed, obviously taking satisfaction in that thought. "Once this steer herd is delivered, and the haying is finished, I'll show Cameron some raiding. So far it's all been one way, but a week from now it'll be different. It won't be just Spade line camps. Before we've finished we'll bust his headquarters to smithereens!"

And then, as he turned his horse eastward, Isham revealed a personal friendliness that surprised Tune. He called, "Take care of yourself, Lew. Those sonsabitches will be gunning for you from now on."

CHAPTER 15

FOR three days, while the sun dried the mud and small dust devils began shirling in the afternoon breeze, Tune rode his patrol without seeing anyone. On the fourth day he remained at Lost Horse until Bob Kiley came in; they renewed their acquaintanceship of three years ago by sharing an early supper.

Middle-aged and inclined to be grouchy, Kiley preferred riding a buckrake in a hayfield. He said, "This is a hell of a way to make a living. You ride alone all day and then eat supper alone."

During the meal they discussed the impending range war and the chances of Anchor winning it.

Kiley, who had gone through the other fight, said, "This might be different, Lew. We might not win it. Cameron has a big crew of toughs and he's ready for a real fight."

"How is he fixed financially?"

"Well, I hear Bart Hayden has throwed in with him. Cameron should have plenty of beef to ship this fall. Tilt tried to get the jump on him by selling a bunch of steers early."

At dusk Tune rode southward, his need for food and companionship appeased. Kiley was right about this patrol riding; it was a poor way to make a living. A soft breeze stirred the grass on Apache Flats and the sky was bright with starlight. A coyote howled on a distant hill, its staccato yammering a wild call of loneliness that threaded the night air like a lament.

Tune wondered if Spade was riding tonight. Angling into the Hoodoo Hills, he keened the darkness for sound of travel. It occurred to him that this late arrival at Beam's camp would fashion a perfect setup for ambush if Spade riders were there ahead of him. He was thinking about that, and preparing to scout the place thoroughly, when he glimpsed the shack's lamplight window.

Lantern light, he thought, remembering that Spade riders had broken his lamp globe the other night.

Someone was in there, or had been in there. Tune drew his gun and eased the pony forward until he was on the edge of the yard. Watching intently, he saw someone pass in front of the light. It occurred to him that Jim Beam had come back, and he thought, *He's making a perfect target.*

Tune angled around until he approached the shack doorway and them called, "That you, Jim?"

A woman came to the doorway and stood framed there with the lantern light behind her and asked, "Lew?"

Astonished, Tune remained beyond the shaft of light. He didn't recognize the voice, and couldn't see her features. Then she called, "It's me—June Patterson."

"I'll be damned," Tune muttered, and riding in, asked, "What are you doing here?"

"Is that how you greet your girl friends after they've ridden miles and miles to see you?" June demanded with mock disappointment. "Aren't you even a little bit glad to see me?"

"Well, yes. But I'm mostly surprised."

As he dismounted June said, "I've been waiting supper for you. I thought you'd be back hours ago."

"How'd you find this place?" Tune asked.

"Indian Joe told me how to get here," June said, adding mischievously, "He's an old customer of Fancy Mayme."

She was, he thought, a frankly brazen female with few inhibitions and no more morals than a mare in heat. Thinking back on her behavior, Tune realized that going to work for Fancy Mayme had been a natural projection of June's impelling need for men.

"This shack is a poor place to be," Tune warned. "No telling when Spade riders will start shooting at it. Bring out the lantern and I'll saddle your horse."

When June came out with the lantern, she complained, "I'm hungry, Lew. I waited all this time so I could eat with you, and now you run me off hungry."

"We'll get something to eat at Indian Joe's place," Tune suggested, masking his annoyance. Saddling her horse hurriedly, Tune helped her into saddle. He said, "Let's get out of here," and led her horse until they were beyond the yard.

As they rode into the comparative safety of timber, he asked, "Why did you come out to see me?"

"Because I like you a lot," she teased. "And I thought you'd be glad to see me, out here alone with no women in sight."

Guessing the real reason for the visit, Tune asked, "Did Hayden refuse to give you the cows?"

"Yes, after he kept me at Spade all night, damn his blarney soul. He finally said my father owned no cows— that he was working for wages. That's a lie, isn't it?"

"Of course, and you can prove it if Frank Paddock and Tate Engle survive this ruckus," Tune said.

June asked, "You'll help me get my inheritance, won't you, Lew?"

"Sure, but it may take some time."

"It'll mean so much to me. I can quit the house and live like a lady—and maybe catch a fine husband before the money gives out."

"Didn't know you were interested in marriage," Tune said.

"Well, I wasn't. But a year in a house makes a girl see things different. It was fun at first. And the pay was good. But a girl gets tired of being with so many men, month in and month out. She gets to wishing she had one man—a husband."

Presently she asked, "Have you ever thought of getting married, Lew?"

"Some."

June was riding close to him—so close that their knees touched, and he was aware of the woman smell of her— some exotic perfume that merged with the scent of pines.

81

He thought, *Two years ago I'd have liked this*. But now his chief reaction to June was annoyance.

She said, "We could camp out—perhaps have a little fire. I think it would be so romantic. I love campfires. And the smell of the pines. There's something about doing it outdoors—you know, close to nature."

"I thought you were hungry," Tune said.

"I mean afterward. After we eat at Indian Joe's place."

Tune kept peering at the trail, kept listening for the rumor of travel. He said, "These hills aren't a safe place to camp. I'll see you to the store, then hit a shuck back. Indian Joe will put you up."

June remained silent for a time. Then she said, "I must say you're not very romantic. This job must have got on your nerves."

"Maybe so," Tune agreed.

"I thought maybe we'd make a pair, you and me. With your cows and mine together we'd have a good start, Lew. We could settle down someplace and be real ranch folks."

When he remained silent, she added, "I like to cook. I'd make you a good wife."

Tune felt sorry for her then. There was nothing really bad about June. She merely had a lust for living, a need for men. She had an easygoing way, he thought, and that was part of her trouble.

"Does the fact I've worked in a house make a difference to you?" June asked.

"Some," Tune admitted, not liking the way this conversation was going.

"But I'm the same girl you used to know," June insisted. "I look the same and act the same. You liked me two years ago."

"Sure," Tune muttered. "But not well enough to marry you."

That triggered June's temper. "You men are all alike," she stormed. "If a girl sleeps with you she's not good enough to marry."

They rode on in silence, and it was close to midnight when they entered the clearing at Tailholt. But there was a light at Indian Joe's store, and presently Tune saw two saddled horses tied to the hitchrack there.

Stopping at once, he said, "Joe's got visitors. This is as far as I go. And if those are Spade riders, don't say you've been traveling with me."

There was an awkward moment while June tried to think

of some way of holding him. But she had already offered the ultimate, and so she said. "Indian Joe will think it odd, me coming into his place unescorted at this time of night."

As Tune turned his horse away, she said quickly, "The least you can do is help me get the cows I inherited."

"That I'll do," Tune promised, and rode off.

The Anchor steers had been choused into the pens at Reservation, a cattle buyer had accepted them, and as was his habit, Tilt Isham had led his dusty crew to Faro Charlie's Saloon. After purchasing a round of drinks and joining in a toast to Anchor, Isham turned to Whitey Melotte and said, "Let's go see Dixon."

As they walked to the sheriff's office, Isham inquired casually, "Have you heard about Beam giving himself up?"

"Hell, no!" Whitey exclaimed, obviously surprised. "You sure about that?"

Isham nodded.

"I never thought he'd do it," Whitey said. "Only last week Indian Joe told me that Beam was about ready to leave the country. Joe said Beam was scared spitless. The damned fool—he'll go to prison sure."

"Maybe," Isham commented. "Maybe not."

They found Dixon sitting with his feet propped on a littered rolltop desk reading a copy of the Tombstone *Epitah*. He said, "I see where John Slaughter is bearing down on the riffraff of Cochise County again. Riley Cameron should have some recruits soon."

As Isham and Melotte took chairs, Dixon asked, "Got your cattle all penned?"

"And sold," Isham said. Then he asked, "What do you think of the Breed Gault deal?"

Dixon grinned. He said, "I asked him to let me see the brand, but he wouldn't. That Tune is a rank Injun, if I ever saw one."

"I've sworn out a warrant with the county attorney for Bart Hayden's arrest on the basis of Breed's confession," Isham said. "I want it served tomorrow."

"But I've got no deputies," Dixon objected. "You've got 'em both out to Anchor."

A note of contempt crept into Isham's voice now; he asked, "Don't you ever ride anything but that swivel chair?"

"You expect Bart Hayden to come in?" Dixon demanded. "You think he'll give himself up, warrant or no warrant?"

"No, but I expect you to serve the warrant regardless," Isham said. "I want it to be official."

Melotte said, "Take a look around Spade while you're out there and let us know what they're doing."

"I ain't going to play spy for nobody," Dixon objected. "By God, you want to get me killed or something? This ain't my fight. It's yours."

Isham asked, "Did you tell Lew Tune that Whitey told you not to look for Jim Beam?"

Dixon glanced at Melotte, then eyed Isham wonderingly. "What's that got to do with Hayden?" he asked.

"Nothing. Did Whitey tell you that?"

Dixon nodded.

For a brief interval then, Isham contemplated Melotte in thoughtful silence, his brown eyes sharply inquisitive. Finally he asked, "How long was it after Tracey Fayette turned you down that you came up with the rustling charge against Beam?"

Melotte attempted to look him in the eye, then glanced at the floor. "Why, I don't recall," he said. "What's that got to do with it?"

"And how long was it after we butchered a steer at Anchor?" Isham asked flatly.

Wholly on the defensive now, Melotte said, "How do you expect me to know that? There's no connection between either of those things with Beam slow-elking an Anchor beef. None at all."

"Isn't there?" Isham hadn't taken his eyes off Melotte. "I didn't think you'd do a thing like that."

"Like what?" Melotte asked.

"Using Anchor to frame Beam for a personal reason— because Miss Fayette accepted him and turned you down."

"Who said I did?" Whitey demanded.

"Lew Tune said so," Isham muttered. "Now I say so."

Something happened to Melotte then, something he couldn't control. "I'll kill that Tune!" he raged. "Him and his long nose!" Then, in a calmer, complaining voice, he said, "Maybe we better drop the charge against Beam. I wouldn't want Tracey to be brought into the case."

"And you wouldn't want to testify to a damned lie, would you?" Isham said in a casual, soothing voice.

Melotte shook his head.

Isham stood up and took a roll of bills from his pocket. Peeling off three, he handed them to Melotte and said, "I consider what you did a disloyal act against Anchor. You're through, as of right now."

Then he turned to Dixon and said, "I'm withdrawing the charge against Beam," and strode out of the office.

CHAPTER 16

THE news traveled fast. Lew Tune, stopping at Indian Joe's store for tobacco two days later, learned that the rustling charge against Beam had been withdrawn, and that Melotte was fired.

"Good on both counts," Tune said, paying for the tobacco. "There's some justice in the world after all."

Spears, who had recited the news as if it were something he had to say quickly, appeared nervous; he took the money and then crossed the room to the plank bar.

Tune asked, "You got hives or something?"

"No—no, I ain't got hives," Indian Joe said.

Tune picked up the paper bag containing six sacks of tobacco. He said, "Never saw you so spooky acting—"

Which was when Whitey Melotte nudged aside the curtain to Spears' living quarters and said sharply, "Now it's my turn, Tune!"

The gun in his hand held Tune motionless. He looked at the tight-lipped expression on Melotte's face and understood that Whitey was primed for murder. It showed in his glinting eyes, and in his voice now as he said, "I told you to keep out of my affairs. But you couldn't keep your big mouth shut. You talked Beam into giving himself up, and that cost me my job. The best goddamn job I ever had."

Only a part of Tune's mind registered Melotte's tirade; mostly he was calculating the distance that separated them —not more than six or seven feet—and deliberately shrugged off the clawing fingers of panic. There was a chance here while Melotte continued to talk; a fragile, thin-raveled chance simply because the little rider wanted to savor his complete mastery of a bigger man. Whitey, Tune thought, was a take-charge galoot and gloried in it. *Otherwise I'd be dead*, Tune thought.

"You ain't talkative now," Melotte jeered. "You're speechless as a thumb-sucking dunce. Ain't you got nothing to say for yourself?"

"Why, yes," Tune said, keeping his voice casual. "Jim Beam is my friend and I got him clear of a rustling charge. Wouldn't you do as much for a friend?"

"You got him clear, all right—and now you're going to pay for it," Whitey snarled.

"Not in here!" Indian Joe objected in a high, nasal voice that was almost a wail. "Tilt Isham will crucify me if it happens in here. Do me a favor, Whitey—take him outside."

That amused Melotte. A grin slackened his lips and he said, "You sound like a blanket squaw with the belly-ache, Joe."

In that instant, as his glance flicked to Spears, Tune flung the paper bag at Melotte's face. Whitey dodged instinctively, and fired as Tune drew his gun. That first bullet, badly aimed because Whitey was dodging as he fired, missed Tune by inches. Tune fired as Whitey's second shot came, those explosions merging. The bullet cut a furrow across Tune's right cheek and took the lobe of his ear with it. Tune saw Melotte teeter back on his heels as if smashed by an invisible fist; he fired again, watched Whitey drop his gun and clutch his chest with both hands.

Melotte fell back against the wall. For a moment he remained in a sitting position, slack-jawed astonishment on his face. Then his clutching hands went limp and he slouched sideways as if too tired to sit up.

Tune holstered his gun. His hand came up to his wounded cheek and gingerly traced the bleeding groove to his ear, fingering its raw tip. He thought sighingly, *That was close.*

"By God, you shouldn't of shot him in here," Indian Joe said.

That complaint drove the last clutch of tension from Tune. The utter ridiculousness of it triggered a burst of uncontrollable laughter during which Tune gasped, "I know —you're a businessman."

Spears eyed him sourly. Looking at Melotte's body, he said, "You killed him, and you're laughing. It ain't fitting."

Sobering abruptly, Tune used a handkerchief to wipe blood from his cheek and neck. He said, "You knew he was waiting to shoot me, but you gave me no sign."

"I don't take sides in these things," Spears said. "Whitey was a customer, same as you."

"And you're a businessman," Tune muttered contemptuously. He wiped his bleeding ear again, then walked over and picked up the paper bag, replacing two sacks of tobacco that had fallen from it. Not looking at Melotte, he went outside to his horse.

"How about the body?" Indian Joe called after him. "What'll I do with it?"

"Suit yourself," Tune said. "He was your customer—not mine."

The next day Jim Beam came back to his place while Tune was out on patrol and found Riley Cameron, with two Spade riders, waiting for him.

"Where do you stand in this fight between Isham and me?" Cameron demanded.

"I'm not in it, one way or the other," Beam said. "I'm strictly neutral."

Spade's owner smiled craftily; he said, "That's how I figured it, Jim. You're too smart to be sucked into a fight that don't concern you."

Beam nodded, and now Cameron said, "I don't want Lew Tune using your place as a line camp. You'll have to tell him to get out."

"But I can't do that," Beam protested. "Lew is an old friend. His cattle are here."

"You'll get rid of him and his cattle or else be raided, the same as any other Anchor line camp. Don't be a sucker for Tune. His number is up, and so is Anchor's. When this is over there won't be any Tune, or any Anchor."

Cameron climbed onto his horse and his two men followed suit. Looking at the pair of riders, who were strangers to him, Beam thought, *They're tough.* The cheek of one of them was bulged with a chew; he squirted tobacco juice close to Beam's boots. Both of them stared at him with a contemptuous, ingrained viciousness that was more expressive than words would have been. They were big outfit riders. He was just a homesteader—one lone man.

"You going to give Tune his walking papers?" Cameron inquired.

Beam nodded.

Watching them ride out of the yard, he lost the last remnant of the pleasures this homecoming had given him. It wouldn't be easy, telling Lew to leave. . . .

He was still thinking about it, and dreading it, when Tune rode in at dusk.

"Welcome home," Tune greeted, and dismounted. "How does it feel to be a free man?"

Standing in the doorway, Beam looked at the raw groove

on Tune's face and the mutilated ear. "What happened to you?" he asked.

"Whitey Melotte and I had a shoot-out at Indian Joe's store," Tune said. "He didn't miss by much."

"And Melotte?"

"I killed him."

Beam kept peering at the wounds, as if they fascinated him. He said, "You came that close to dying."

"Close don't count," Tune said mockingly. He asked again, "How does it seem to be back and free?"

"Well, it was good—until this afternoon. Riley Cameron and two of his toughs were here when I pulled in. They were waiting for me."

"So?"

Beam gave his attention to building a cigarette. Not looking at Tune, he blurted, "Riley said you'd have to leave."

"That's like him," Tune reflected. "Riley likes to play God."

He waited for Beam to say more on the subject, but Jim muttered, "I'll get supper," and turned away.

Tune led his horse to the corral. Unsaddling it, he thought, *Jim spooks easily*. Afterward, forking hay to the horses, he tried to understand Beam, and could not. What was it that made a man afraid to be a man, he wondered, that caused him to allow other men to push him around without fighting back? Being pushed around was for nesters with wives and children to think about. Jim had no family, yet he was thinking as if he and Tracey were already married—as if he had youngsters around the place. *That's what marriage does to a man*, Tune thought, and felt sorry for Jim Beam.

It was dark now and Beam had lit the lantern. Tune walked out beyond the lean-to; he stopped to listen, standing perfectly still for several moments before continuing on. There was no moon, but starlight kept the night's darkness from being opaque; it gave form and substance to the brush. Tune circled the yard, stopping at intervals to listen. Off to the east a cow bellowed, and he wondered if that were one of his. He would have to make arrangements with Isham to move his stuff onto Anchor range, now that he was no longer welcome here. It occurred to Tune that he was in no hurry to join Beam in the shack, that this reunion didn't mean much to him. Recalling how it had been before, when they had got together frequently in Reservation, Tune thought, *Jim has changed*.

Now Beam came to the doorway and called, "Supper's ready."

Tune went in, and they ate in silence for a time. Then Beam said, "Why don't you sell your cattle and pull out of this country, Lew? You're single. There's nothing to hold you here?"

"But there is," Tune explained. "I'm beholden to Tilt Isham for saving my life, and I've got to pay off Bart Hayden for the deaths of my Mexicans."

Beam looked at him questioningly. He asked, "Are either of those things worth risking your life for? You've come as close as any man ever came to being killed. If Melotte's bullet had been a sixteenth of an inch to the left you'd have died."

Tune thought about this while he cleaned up his plate. How could he explain his feelings about such things as life and death when he wasn't sure himself how he felt about them? Finally he said, "Maybe we look at things different, Jim. I figure we've all got to die someday. We were sentenced to death the day we were born. Fretting about it won't make much difference. When it's your turn to go, you'll die. *Quien sabe*, as the Mexicans say—who knows?"

"But there's no point in asking for it," Beam insisted, "which is what you're doing."

Tune shrugged. He said, "Speaking of asking for it, I'd better go outside and look around while you wash the dishes. Then we'll tote our blankets into the brush."

Afterward, when they were bedded down a quarter of a mile from the shack, Tune asked, "When are you and Tracey going to get married?"

"Next spring," Beam said. "Tracey believes in long engagements. And even after that she'll stay in town and continue to run the restaurant until I get enough money ahead to build a decent house."

Tune thought, *A hell of a way to start married life.* To his way of thinking, a bride should go with her husband regardless; she should share his life for better or worse. . . .

The next morning when Tune rode toward Lost Horse, his blanket roll was tied behind the cantle, his saddlebags were crammed with cooking utensils, and he was leading two Anchor horses. Beam had expressed regret at the parting. He had said, "This is a hell of a thing, Lew—running you off this way." But Tune sensed that Jim's primary feeling was one of relief.

The air had a crisp coolness with a smell of fall in it;

as the sun climbed higher, an autumn haze put its smoky blur on the far hills. Tune thought, *Coming early.*

When he came within sight of the line camp, he saw that several saddled horses were tied to the corral fence; coming closer, he glimpsed men sitting on the stoop as if waiting for him. Tune pulled up, quite sure they were Anchor riders, but wanting to be real sure before he went any farther. Presently, as he waited, indecisive and wary, he saw a man walk toward the corral. This one mounted a pony and came loping toward Tune, who then rode ahead and soon identified Tilt Isham.

As they met, Isham said, "You've got your horses and your blankets. Beam run you off?"

Tune nodded. "Cameron called on him yesterday and suggested he put the boots to me."

As they rode toward camp, Isham said, "It's just as well. It's our turn to do some raiding now." Then he added, "I hear you and Whitey had a showdown."

"He jumped me, Tilt—it was him or me," Tune explained.

When the extra horses had been corraled, Tune joined the group in front of the dugout—John Brite, Larry Clawson, Pete Maroney and Bob Kiley. They seemed strangely subdued, yet there was a sense of excitement here, and Tune thought, *This is the start of something.*

When he had hunkered on his heels in the dust, Isham said, "I've already told these boys how it's to be. Now I'll tell you. I sent Larry over to scout Spade last week. He says there's four men riding day and night patrol at Willow Spring. The only time all four of them get together is for breakfast, about daylight. The same thing at Cameron's North Camp—four more men. Larry got through them and found another bunch in a roundup camp on Mexican Mesa. That's why Cameron has those patrols working day and night—he's afraid we'll jump his beef gather. He evidently wants to sell some steers early, same as I did.

"The plan is this. We'll ride easy through the Hoodoos, giving the night patrol time to pull in for breakfast. Then we hit 'em—and afterward hole up there most of the day, resting and eating Spade groceries."

"What's after Willow Spring?" Tune asked.

"We play the same game at North Camp, jumping them the next morning. After that there's nothing betwixt us and the roundup. I want to bust that up real good. First we'll set 'em afoot by running off the *remuda*—then we'll scatter those steers to hell and gone."

They all thought about it in silence, until John Brite asked, "How many men at the roundup camp?"

"I tallied fourteen, including the horse wrangler," Clawson said.

"You reckon six of us can handle that many?" Brite asked.

"We can cause them considerable trouble," Isham said. He took off his hat and scratched his head; he smoothed his rust-brown hair and added, "I want to set 'em afoot, and maybe put three or four out of business. They aren't cowpunchers, strictly speaking—they're gunhawks. Tombstone scum run off by John Slaughter. We can't whip Spade all at once, but we can whittle 'em down, *poco-a-poco*—little by little."

Bob Kiley glanced at Tune and grinned; he said, "Anyway, this beats patrol riding."

"It beats anything in the work line I know of," Pete Maroney suggested, a note of suppressed excitement in his voice. "A man could live his whole life without having a chance to hunt two-legged polecats like them Spade bastards."

And Larry Clawson said soberly, "I want to knock off at least two of them to make up for Jack Medwick. He didn't even have a gun in his hand when they killed him."

Bob Kiley got up, glanced at Tune's face and inquired, "Did Whitey do that with a bullet?"

Tune nodded.

They all peered at his face then, and Kiley said, "He couldn't have missed by much less. I'll warm up the coffee and frijoles."

Presently, as Tune was getting a drink of water from the *olla* suspended from the dugout's overhang, Isham said, "Rider coming yonderly."

Tune satified his thirst before peering out at the horseman coming across the flats. He watched him for a brief interval, then said, "There's only one man I know who slouches on a horse like an Injun with belly cramps. That's Keno Smith, by grab."

He walked out a short distance to meet Smith, wholly pleased at this reunion. As Smith came in, Tune said, "About time you were showing up."

"You're a hard galoot to catch up with," Smith complained. "I stayed at Indian Joe's place last night and was asaddle before daylight. But when I got to Beam's, he said you didn't live there any more."

Tune shook his hand, said, "Light down and join the merry throng."

Isham revealed his pleasure at this unexpected addition to Anchor forces by saying, "If I'd had my druthers, there isn't a man I'd rather have with us than you, Keno."

That pleased Smith, whose bearded face eased into a cherubic smile. "When does the big shindig start?" he asked.

"Tonight," Isham said. "We'll be riding soon as we eat."

Smith's marble-bright eyes twinkled and he said, "I arrived just in the nick of time." Then, as he got out his pipe and tobacco, he added, "Breed Gault won't kill any more Mexicans. He's dead."

"Dead?" Tune prompted.

"Somebody came to his cell window couple nights ago and shot him twice in the face. Bart Hayden, I suppose, so Breed wouldn't testify against him in court."

The news that the man he had branded was dead, sobered Tune. He said, "Breed deserved killing, but not that way, thinking Hayden had come to help him break out. That's how it was, most likely—Hayden calling Breed to the window and then giving it to him."

"Exactly," Smith agreed. "They said Breed had powder stains on his face."

Afterward, when they had eaten and were riding west across Apache Flats, Keno said to Tune, "All I ask for is one clean shot at Bart Hayden."

"No," Tune muttered. "He's mine."

CHAPTER 17

LATE afternoon sunlight filtered through the pines as Tilt Isham and his six-man crew rode through the Hoodoo Hills. There was no hurry. They were like hunters starting out and not yet in game country; they talked, and laughed occasionally, and were at ease.

Keno Smith was jubilant. He said, "By God, it's good to be astraddle of a horse again. Riding a bed makes a man get snuffy."

Tune, too, reacted to the companionship of other men after lone patrol riding. This was good. There was a definite task to be accomplished, a goal to be reached. It reminded him of the old days in the cavalry when the troops had ridden out, after the monotony of post duty.

They were approaching a high meadow when Keno said abruptly, "Somebody coming yonderly."

The crew pulled up, and Isham asked, "Where?"

Tune peered ahead, seeing nothing, but Smith said, "He just came off that ridge beyond the meadow."

Tune still didn't see anything. However, he had a high regard for Smith's keen eyes, and so he suggested, "Maybe we'd better bush up, Tilt. It might be a Spade patrol."

They deployed then, Isham and his men going off the trail on one side, Tune and Smith on the other. When they were well back in the brush, Tune asked, "What did you see, Keno?"

"Sunlight glancing off metal," Smith said. "Saw it twice, and the second time it was nearer."

They had waited about five minutes when a rider came into the meadow. Apparently he was following this same trail, for he came on at a walk, crossing the clearing and entering the timber on this side.

As the rider came close, Tune identified him as being Baldy Crouch and was amused at the thought that Baldy was going to be captured for the second time. Crouch seemed to sense surveillance now; he peered about, as if aware of the eyes watching him but not knowing where they were. A Winchester was cradled across his left arm; he was like that when Anchor riders swarmed out, surrounding him.

Surprise and dismay tightened Baldy's face; he sat locked in abject immobility as Tilt Isham disarmed him. No one had spoken during this swift encirclement. Now Tune said casually, "Nice to see you again so soon, Baldy. How's your head?"

Crouch ignored him. He said to Isham, "I'm just riding. I was going to Indian Joe's for supper."

"Just riding—and spying," Isham said.

Bob Kiley asked, "You want him tied, boss?" and when Isham nodded, Kiley bound Baldy's hands and tied them to the saddlehorn. When he picked up the pony's reins, the group continued its leisurely way westward.

Presently Isham asked, "You working out of the Willow Spring camp?"

Baldy nodded, whereupon Isham said, "Maybe you're lucky."

"You going to raid it?" Crouch asked.

Isham said, "Yes," and now Pete Maroney added, "We ain't figgerin' to take no more prisoners."

Bart Hayden ate supper alone in the main house kitchen, served by Riley Cameron's Mexican housekeeper. He was in charge of Spade headquarters during Riley's absence at the roundup and had exercised his proprietorship by establishing day and night patrols to guard the place against possible Anchor attack. But inactivity for the past two days was having its effect on him; finished eating, he eyed the Mexican woman with an interest spawned by boredom.

Maria, he knew, was Riley's mistress as well as housekeeper. Looking her over now, he judged her age to be about thirty; she had a brunette prettiness that had a certain appeal despite the fact she was more buxom than Hayden liked his women to be. When she poured him a second cup of coffee, he said, "Maria, *querida,*" and placed an arm about her hips.

The women finished pouring the coffee before she said, "Riley won't like you," and drew away from him. But his male attention had pleased her, and she showed it in the sloe-eyed smile she gave him. "I think Riley comes home tonight."

Aroused by the musk-scented, woman smell of her, Hayden said, "If he doesn't, I'll keep you company, Maria, so you won't be lonesome."

Maria placed the coffeepot on the stove. She said again, "Riley won't like you."

"He won't know anything about it," Hayden promised. "It'll be a secret between us." He gulped down the rest of his coffee and invited, "Come over here."

Maria shook her head. She stood placidly watching as he got up and came across the kitchen. When he grabbed for her, she evaded him, and reaching under her skirt, drew a stiletto from a garter. "I am Riley's woman," she said calmly. "Not yours."

"So you're a hellcat," Hayden said, his appetite sharpened by her reluctance to accept his advances. He smiled at her, his amber eyes glinting. "I'm especially fond of hellcats."

Maria backed up so that she was against a wall. Excitement heightened the color in her swarthy cheeks and she

94

watched him with a half-smile on her lips as if this were a game she enjoyed.

"Worst I'll get is a cut on the arm," Hayden said with a confidence born of his rising passion. "Then I'll take the knife away from you, and we'll have fun together. "

Maria held the stiletto so that lamplight gleamed on its blade; she said, "It is sharp, señor—it will cut deep."

But Hayden laughed, all his amorous instincts aroused; he was stepping toward her in the stealthy fashion of a man stalking a loose horse, when Riley Cameron came to the kitchen doorway and inquired, "What's going on?"

Hayden halted at once. He shrugged, and turning to Cameron, said casually, "I was trying to make friends with your Mexican woman."

Riley came into the kitchen and hung his hat on a nail. "You ain't the first," he said. "Maria has carved up several jaspers that had the same notion." Without his hat, the monk's fringe of gray hair on either side of his bald pate made him look older; it emphasized his big nose and formed a contrast for the steel-black bristle of whiskers on his gaunt cheeks. He took a chair at the table and said, "Git me some supper, *muy pronto.*"

"*Si,*" Maria acknowledged. Hoisting her dress, she replaced the stiletto in the garter on her right thigh, then busied herself at the stove.

"Nice legs," Bart said admiringly. "Real nice."

Cameron chuckled. "When I pick a woman, she's a good one. Nice all over. I've had Maria for ten years, and don't have to worry none about stray studs. She's an artist with that knife."

Hayden joined Cameron at the table. He said jokingly, "We're partners, ain't we—share and share alike?"

"Not the woman," Cameron said. "She's my personal property."

Maria brought them both coffee, and Cameron said, "We've finished the gather, and they start out at daylight tomorrow. We'll push your pool steers up near Willow Spring tomorrow and meet the trail herd day after tomorrow."

"How many you got gathered?" Hayden asked.

"Better'n four hundred. That means we'll have about a thousand head all told when we leave Willow Spring. I want plenty of men with the cattle. I'll pull in the patrols and only leave four men here. The rest of us will be with the herd."

"I can't ride into town," Hayden said. "There's a warrant out for me, remember?"

"I got a job all picked out for you," Cameron said. "I want to set up a sort of headquarters at Beam's place." That reminded him of something humorous; he said in a teasing, chuckling way, "When I think how we rode most of a wet night to empty our guns into Beam's empty shack—"

"To hell with that!" Hayden snapped. "How was I to know Tune wasn't in there." Cameron's reference to that night triggered a raging sense of failure. He said, "I'll get Tune if it's the last thing I ever do."

"I don't like him either," Cameron muttered. "Well, you can start off at Beam's place with four men, then when we finish the drive we'll put a bunch in there. It's a good spot. Plenty of water, and close enough to Anchor so we can give Isham fits."

"That reminds me—your man Mascarat pulled in this afternoon with seven riders he hired in Tombstone," Hayden reported.

"How do they look?"

Hayden shrugged. "Guns with ears. What does your crew add up to now?"

"Let's see. I had twenty-three men on the payroll when this thing started. We lost Bascom and Taber. That made twenty-one. Then Carson and Tevitson cashed in at the Anchor roundup camp fight, which left nineteen. Then Breed got hisself arrested—and you took care of him. Eighteen and seven gives us twenty-five, not counting you, me or your two men and the boy."

"Twenty-nine and a half," Hayden mused. "That's a lot of guns."

Maria brought Cameron's supper, which he attacked with the enthusiasm of a hungry man.

Hayden asked, "How much country does Anchor control?"

"Everything from the Pena Blancas to the Las Jarillas east and west, and north beyond Fresno Springs to the Tumacacoris."

Hayden whistled. "That's a hell smear of real estate," he said. "Must be three or four times more than you've got now."

"Sure, but have you thought what all that country added to what I've got will mean?" Cameron asked. He bolted some food, then said, "We'll have a real spread, friend Bart—a real big spread."

Cameron's chalky eyes glinted in the lamplight and his lips, almost feminine in their fullness, were loosely pursed. At this moment, as a smiling anticipation creased his cheeks, Riley Cameron was the personification of raw greed—of the acquisitiveness that had roweled him so long and so relentlessly.

"It's taken me twenty years," he reflected, his voice little more than a whisper. "I never had the cash for a long fight before, but I've got it now."

"You mean we've got it," Hayden corrected.

Cameron nodded. "Cash and men aplenty. All we got to do is lick Tilt Isham and his crew. Then we'll have a goddamn cattle empire that'll take us four days to ride across."

Maria brought more coffee; she served the two men with a sloe-eyed smile that invited attention. But the men didn't notice her.

Tilt Isham's crew had halted at sundown and made a campfire. Three coffeepots, including Tune's, were placed on the coals, and afterward the men ate a frugal supper. They talked and laughed, and ignored Crouch, who wolfed his food in silence.

Later, Isham held his watch to the firelight and said, "We'll mosey along now."

He led them though the dark hills with an instinctive sense of direction that increased Tune's admiration for Anchor's boss. Tilt, he thought, was no swivel-chair ramrod; he knew this country the only way a man can really know a country—by riding it day and night. Later, as they crossed a starlit crest, Isham said, "Pine Top Spring down there. Remember it, Lew?"

"Yeah—real good," Tune said, and marveled at the changes that had occurred since the last time he had ridden this high country. He would have laughed at the thought he'd end up riding for Anchor.

A cold breeze swept this high elevation, causing Tune to turn up his mackinaw collar to protect chilled ears. When the trail finally dropped down to timber again, the wind ceased and the cold was less intense. Tune was riding, half asleep, when Isham said, "Willow Spring is about a mile ahead. We stop here for coffee."

Presently, with a fire going, they all stood close, soaking

97

up its heat. Crouch held his bound hands to the flames; he said, "If you'd turn me loose, Mr. Isham, I'd leave the country. Honest, I've had enough."

Isham peered at him, his firelit face entirely grave. He said, "Not now—but I'll keep it in mind."

Warm now, and drowsy, the men drank their coffee in reflective silence. Gone was the cheerfulness that had graced their supper fire. This was more than the beginning of a new day, Tune thought; it was the start of something that would last a long time. And some of these men might not live to see it finished.

Isham said, "Pete, John and Larry, ease around to that ridge behind the camp. We'll spread out in front of it. I'll give them a warning shot—after that we'll pour lead into that cabin."

As the three men rode off, Isham scooped dirt onto the fire. He said, "We'll go up a bit closer and leave our ponies. Also our prisoner."

Dawn was diluting night's blackness when they rode away from the dead campfire.

CHAPTER 18

THERE was a light in the cabin, and now as daybreak came, a fragile ribbon of smoke rose from the stovepipe. Presently a man came out carrying a bucket. He walked twenty yards to the pump and filled the bucket, the rasping complaint of the pump handle sounding loud against the dawn's frosty stillness.

Isham asked, "Reckon you could put a bullet through that bucket, Keno?"

"Sure," Smith said and took careful aim as the man walked back toward the cabin.

The rifle's report brought the man's head snapping around, his eyes briefly scrutinizing these trees; then, as water spurted from a hole in the bucket, he ran into the cabin and closed the door.

"That's warning enough," Isham said, and put a bullet through the window.

All the guns opened up, their multiple reports merging into a prolonged racket as bullets smashed the cabin's front and rear windows and splintered the board door. The men in the line camp were firing now, their bullets thudding into roundabout trees; but they had no targets and their random shooting was merely token resistance.

Baldy Crouch, tied to a tree back with the horses, listened to the continued firing and was content to be a prisoner. The three men in the cabin, he thought, were doomed.

During a reloading lull a man came out through the back window and ran toward the corral. He had traversed half the distance when Pete Maroney fired at him. The bullet's impact turned him halfway around, and he dropped his gun; but he made another effort to reach the corral, running doubled over, his boots churning up a plume of dust.

"You're hard to convince," Maroney muttered. He fired again, and missed; then, as all three Anchor guns blasted in unison, the man went down.

"That's one for Jack Medwick," John Brite said in a voice high-pitched with excitement.

No more shots came from the cabin.

Finally Tune said, "I think they're done, Tilt."

"Might be playing possum," Isham suggested.

They waited out another five minutes. Then Isham said, "Bob, bring up the horses."

Faint sunlight was creeping across the westward ridge when they rode slowly toward the cabin with Baldy Crouch in tow. Maroney, Brite and Clawson came off the ridge and angled warily around the cabin's north end where there were no windows. Isham warned, "Don't bunch up—spread out."

And now Tune said, "I'll take a look-see."

But Isham said at once, "I'll do it." He rode quickly to the door and opened it; when the others came up he said, "One dead and one wounded."

The wounded man, whom Crouch identified as Tex Slater, cradled a bullet-shattered arm and whimpered, "I'm bleeding to death!"

Tune used the man's neckerchief to fashion a tourniquet above the elbow. He said, "Keep it twisted tight," and then used a flour sack as a bandage.

Later, when the two bodies had been buried and Bob Kiley was cooking breakfast, Crouch came up to Isham and said, "Let me take Slater to a doctor in town—then I'll keep going."

While Isham considered the request, Crouch said urgently, "Spade is a goddamn ragtag outfit. I never did like Cameron, and I don't aim to die for him."

99

"All right," Isham said. "But if we catch you again, you're a gone gosling."

As if fearing that Isham might change his mind, Crouch quickly saddled a horse for Slater and helped him into saddle. . . .

After breakfast the Anchor Crew rode up into the pines and slept until late in the afternoon.

When Cameron, Hayden and four punchers had the pool steers within eight miles of Willow Spring, Riley said, "I'll ride into camp and tell them they've got company for supper."

He rode on, well pleased with the way things were going. The Mexican Mesa roundup would soon be here; after that, with twenty five men guarding the merged herds, they could trail the cattle into Reservation without much chance of trouble from Anchor.

Cameron grinned, thinking of the money a thousand head of steers would bring, and what that money would accomplish. For the first time in twenty years he was in a position to lick Anchor—to be the big mogul of this range. It occurred to him that Bart Hayden might not be the most congenial partner a man might choose. Bart had a bossy, arrogant way with him. But that could be taken care of after Anchor was smashed.

At first, as he rode into camp, Cameron wasn't aware that anything was amiss; he was on his way to the corral when he came to the freshly filled grave. Then he noticed the cabin's shattered rear window—and knew at once that Anchor had raided the place.

He thought, *On their way to Mexican Mesa!* But when he scouted the yard, he observed the fresh horse tracks leading back into the pines.

Cameron rode up to the open doorway and glanced into the cabin, noting the signs of seige, the bloodstains on the floor. "I've got four less riders," he muttered. "Goddamn Tilt Isham!"

Riding back toward the herd, Cameron wondered why Isham and his men hadn't kept going toward the roundup camp. The puzzle of it nagged at his mind; there was something here that didn't seem right. He stopped and looked back at the camp. Isham had attacked the place with several riders; why had he turned back for no apparent reason?

Cameron rode on, unable to find a logical explanation.

He was passing through brush two miles from Willow Spring cabin when something caused him to glance back again—to see seven riders emerge from the pines. Halting his horse, he watched them come to the line-camp corral and dismount, wondering what they were up to. Then it occurred to him that they were intending to eat supper there, before continuing on toward Mexican Mesa.

It was dusk now, and Bob Kiley's supper fire gave off the appetizing odors of frying steak and frijoles bubbling in an iron pot as big as a bucket. The horses had been fed and the men were lounging in the dust before the cabin doorway.

A sense of pleasant relaxation pervaded the camp, yet Lew Tune felt uneasy. He got up and circled the cabin, instinctively ranging beyond the back window's shaft of lamplight. He thought, *I'm spooky,* and guessed it was because of what had happened at Beam's place. When he went back to the group in front of the cabin, Isham asked, "Something bothering you, Lew?"

Tune shrugged. "Guess it's just the idea of a lamplit camp being a trap," he said.

"Most of Spade's crew are at Mexican Mesa," Isham said.

Bob Kiley came to the doorway and stood there, framed in lamplight. "Supper'll be ready in about twenty minutes," he announced.

Tune couldn't relax. He got up and went to the corral where the horses, still saddled, were munching their hay. A cool breeze sifted down from the high hills, and off to the south a cow bellowed plaintively. Tune was tightening his cinch, intending to take a little *pasear* around the camp, when there was a blast of gunfire out front—a terrific, concentrated merging of reports that was immediately followed by a drumbeat of hooves.

Spade! Tune thought and saw the light blink out of the cabin's rear window. In the moment while he stood there astonished, ragged spurts of muzzle flame flared in the yonder darkness. He had fired twice at those beacons when indistinct shapes charged toward the corral. Maroney came rushing up, shouting, "Pull out—pull out!" in a queerly frantic voice.

And now Keno Smith, moving in beside Tune, cautioned, "Don't shoot—you'll give 'em targets."

A moment later there was another burst of gunfire out

front and the staccato beat of horses galloping past the cabin. Then Isham loomed up, supporting Larry Clawson. He said, "Help me get Larry on a horse."

Tune helped boost Clawson into saddle, his hands coming in contact with blood. Clawson groaned once and collapsed, and Isham said, "Hold him till I get asaddle."

Now Tune heard Maroney complain, "My right arm is broke. Somebody tighten this cinch."

Spade riders were still firing at the cabin, still riding there, and presently a man shouted, "Out back—the corral!"

Almost as once there was a rush of horses and a bullet splintered a corral rail close to Tune.

The rest of it was utter confusion, with cursing men fighting spooked horses, with the taint of gunsmoke and hoof-churned dust making an acrid stench in the darkness.

Getting into saddle, Tune asked, "Where's Kily and Brite?"

"Dead," Isham muttered. "Shot to doll ribbons."

As they moved out, Tune rode on the other side of Clawson, leading his horse while Isham supported the unconscious rider. They were leaving the yard when they almost collided with a Spade rider who fired point-blank. Isham's horse went down, and as the Spade man fired again, Tune slammed two fast shots into that indistinct shape and saw it tip over as the horse went lunging past him.

Tune caught Clawson as he was falling from saddle; he said, "Climb up behind Larry, Tilt."

Isham was slow getting up. He grunted a curse as he finally made it, and Tune asked, "You hurt?"

"Some," Isham muttered.

Smith and Maroney had gone on, their dim shapes melting into the yonder darkness. Spade was still firing at the cabin and at the corral, and Tune thought, *We've got a chance.*

CHAPTER 19

THEY rode through the pines at a walk, stopping frequently to listen. Smith and Maroney were somewhere ahead of them; in this quilted darkness they would be riding slow, too, Tune thought. Once he heard what sounded like a shod hoof clanging against rock. He said, "Wait," but there was no sound save the sighing of the high pines.

102

They angled out of the timber, quartering into the Apache Flats trail and following it eastward. Soon after that Tune noticed the smell of risen dust and knew that riders had passed here moments ago. Was it Keno and Pete—or Spade?

Starlight made it less dark here on the flats; sometime after midnight a fingernail crescent of moon rose, faintly illuminating the roundabout brush.

"We'll stop at Rojo Seep," Isham muttered. "That's the nearest water."

"Water?" Tune asked.

"Clean and bandage Larry's wound," Isham said, biting off his words as if it were an effort to speak. "Mine, too."

Tune understood then that Isham was hurt worse than he had let on. He said, "Let's swap horses, Tilt, and I'll hang onto Larry."

The transfer was made, Isham taking a little time to get back into saddle but making no complaint. Clawson was an inert weight against Tune's arms. When they stopped briefly to listen for sound or pursuit, Tune placed his palm over Clawson's down-tilted face and could feel no breath against his hand. They negotiated a rocky slope, the horses clawing for footing and Isham cursing morosely when his pony stumbled. Soon after that he said, "This is it."

Tune lifted Clawson out of saddle, then foraged for firewood. When he came back Isham was lying beside Clawson; his eyes were closed and Tune thought he had passed out. But presently, as Tune got a fire going, Isham said, "We won't need to wash Larry's wound. He's dead."

Tilt was sitting up now, his firelit face tightly drawn and pale, the front of his mackinaw soaked with blood. Tune filled a skillet with water from the seep and put it on the fire; then he asked, "Bullet go through you, Tilt?"

Isham shook his head. "Still in there."

Tune wondered how that could be, for the Spade rider had fired point-blank when he knocked down Isham's horse and his second shot hit Tilt. Tune said, "At that close range it should've gone right through you."

"No, I got it out in front of the cabin," Isham explained. "A nearly spent bullet. But it knocked me down. I was lucky to get out of there with Larry."

That astonished Tune. Isham had been wounded all the time. Remembering Pete Maroney's frantic announcement that his arm was broken, Tune thought, *Isham was hurt worse and said nothing.*

Peeling back the mackinaw and shirt, Tune saw that the

103

bullet had penetrated Isham's left side between the hip and the rib cage. He said, "Must've broken a rib or two."

Isham nodded, keeping his lips tight clamped as Tune cleansed the wound. Tune used a sleeve of his own shirt for a bandage and bound it tight with Isham's belt. Tilt's teeth were chattering when it was finished. Tune buttoned his blood-sogged shirt and mackinaw and said, "Lay close to the fire and dry out."

Isham drank his coffee slowly, as if savoring its warmth and flavor. He said, "I'll be laid up for a while, Lew. I'd like to have you run the crew—what there is left of it."

"*Bueno*," Tune said, He glanced at Clawson, dreading the thought of touching him again. Why was it, he wondered, that the living disliked handling the dead? Finally he asked, "What do we do with Larry?"

"Tote him to Anchor," Isham said. "He deserves a decent grave."

When they moved out again, Isham was riding in front of Tune who led the pony bearing Clawson's body lashed to the saddle. Isham said, "This is some different than I thought it would be." Soon after that he slumped, passed out or asleep.

At daylight, Tune observed the fresh tracks of four or five horses in the trail. Those Spade riders, he guessed, must have aimed straight for Anchor while he and Isham were maneuvering through the pines. But now, in daylight, they would double-back and start circling, looking for some tracks to follow.

So tired that thinking was an effort, Tune sat there in the trail for upwards of five minutes, trying to decide where to go. Anchor, now, was out of the question. If he could make it across Apache Flats to the Big Meadow hay camp, there would be a wagon to place Isham in, and men to escort it. But Spade hunters could see for miles on these flats. If they sighted him, there would be no chance of escape. Finally deciding to head into the Hoodoo Hills, Tune pulled off the trail and soon rode up a canyon between wooded ridges. It was just a matter of time, he thought, until more Spade riders would be trailing him.

Past noon he reached the edge of the malpais strip and rode south for more than three miles before turning east. The horses would leave little if any sign of their passing on this flinty rock, and that might mean the difference between escape and capture. He thought, *Capture hell*. Spade would give no quarter to him or Tilt Isham.

104

The horse, toting a double load, was tired. Riding at a monotonous, plodding walk, Tune fought off an inclination to doze, and he lost all track of time. Isham groaned occasionally, but did not regain consciousness. Later, after they had left the malpais and were passing through a thicket of young pines, Tune heard a man shout, "No tracks here." Wide-awake now, Tune halted, and hoped his horses wouldn't nicker. He glimpsed a rider threading his way through timber a hundred yards north of him, and had a bad two minutes until that man passed on. Afterward he waited out a long interval of silence before continuing eastward.

At sundown Tune stopped beside a high rock reef, maneuvered Isham to the ground, and covered him with a blanket. He built a small fire, made coffee and fried some bacon. Tilt awoke and accepted coffee, but wouldn't eat, saying that he was sick at his stomach.

Speaking in the jerky, abrupt way of a man under the pressure of pain, Isham said, "We've got to keep—Spade's steer herd—from reaching Reservation."

Tune nodded agreement, and then Isham explained, "Cameron's credit no good—at the bank. Doesn't market those steers—runs out of money. That scum will quit if no payday. Won't fight for free."

"We'll stop the steers," Tune promised.

There was no water for the horses, but Tune picketed them where they could graze on sparse grass. When he came back to the fire, Isham was asleep, his breathing shallow and irregular. Tune lay down beside him; he thought, *I'll sleep for an hour.* It was dawn when he awoke, so cold and stiff he could scarcely move.

Near noon Tune watered the horses at Pine Top Spring. There were fresh tracks here, telling him that Spade had scouted this country within the past hour or so—perhaps within the past few minutes. He rode into the timber, reined in behind a windfall and remained there, listening intently, for upwards of fifteen minutes before riding on. Some time after that Isham roused himself and asked, "Where are we?"

"About ten miles from Tailholt," Tune said. "How you feel?"

"Thirsty," Isham said. "Burning up."

He fumbled with the canteen which Tune had filled at the spring, took a long drink and passed the canteen to Tune. Presently he asked, "Why Tailholt?"

"We'll get a wagon from Indian Joe—tote you to town so Doc Snyder can dig that slug out of you."

Isham grunted acceptance of that plan. He remained erect for a few minutes, then went limp. When he roused again he mumbled incoherently, and Tune thought, *He's delirious.*

Shortly after that Keno Smith quartered into the trail directly ahead of them and said, "I been looking for you?"

"Where's Maroney?" Tune inquired.

"Gone to town to get patched up. That arm was giving him fits."

Smith contemplated Tune for a moment before adding, "You look beat, Lew. Climb down and I'll spell you."

When they had changed mounts, Smith said, "They raided Anchor last night—burned it to the ground."

That news shocked Tune. He asked, "What happened to the men there?"

"Killed or run off. There's a bunch of Spade riders staying at Jim Beam's place. They've been combing the hills for you, I guess."

They rode in silence for a time, while Tune absorbed the full import of what Keno had told him. It seemed almost impossible that Anchor could have fallen in so short a time. He asked, "How about the men at the hay camp?"

"Well, I saw a big smoke over there yesterday afternoon. Suppose they burned the haystacks. When Spade jumped us at Willow Spring, they got the upper hand and played it fast. Everything happened just right for them. And now we're licked."

Keno glanced at the body lashed to the led horse, asked, "Why tote that around?"

"Well, Tilt wants Clawson to have a decent grave. Suppose we better take his body into town also."

"Damned nonsense," Keno grumbled. "There's nothing more useless than a dead man. He's just so much garbage."

At dusk, when they were close to Tailholt, Tune rode ahead, scouting Spears' store before signaling Smith in. He told Indian Joe what they needed—hot water, a bandage, a wagon and a meal.

"In that order," Tune said, "and *muy pronto*."

"But I—" Indian Joe began.

"But nothing, goddamn it!" Tune said rankly. "We're paying customers and we want fast service. Get some hot water out back in a hurry, and bring a lantern."

Then Tune filled a wagon bed with hay and helped Smith lift Isham into it. Anchor's boss groaned as Tune cleansed his wound and put on a fresh bandage. "He's lost an awful lot of blood," Tune muttered. "Maybe too much." He covered Isham with a blanket, then Clawson's body was placed in the wagon and a tarp drawn over them.

"Take off," Tune told Indian Joe.

Sometime before midnight a crescent moon rose; after that Tune and Smith left the trail, flanking the wagon at some distance on either side and stopping frequently to listen for sound of travel behind them. As the hours passed without sign of trouble, Tune thought, *We're winning this deal.* Near dawn the air turned so cold that the horses' breath made puffs of vapor in the frosty moonlight. When they approached Reservation, Tune rode ahead to awaken Doc Snyder and arrange for Isham's hotel room.

CHAPTER **20**

SHERIFF Jeff Dixon was as worried as a man could be. At first, when Baldy Crouch had brought Tex Slater into town and told about the Willow Spring shooting, it appeared that Isham was getting the best of this Anchor-Spade feud. But yesterday Pete Maroney had ridden in with a bullet-shattered arm and told about Isham being ambushed at Willow Spring. Then Dixon's two deputies had come in with the unbelievable story of Anchor's burning after four of Isham's men had been killed. Last night Big Joe Walsh and Jack Mabry had come in with news that the hay camp had been raided. Now Tilt Isham was at the Palace Hotel, in what Doc Snyder called a dying condition. All of which meant that he, a politician who took pride in his prudence, had backed the wrong side. Spade would be the big outfit in this country from now on.

Dixon usually didn't drink before supper, but now he stood at Faro Charlie's bar and downed a double shot of bourbon. "I never thought Riley Cameron would lick Anchor so bad, so soon," he muttered. "It don't scarcely seem possible."

"I wonder who Riley will run for sheriff," Faro Charlie reflected, wanting to needle this star-packer who usually chose the right side.

Dixon eyed the saloonman with irritation. He said, "I've been at it too long to quit now, Charlie. I'm too damned old to go back to punching cows for a living."

Keno Smith, Big Joe Walsh and Jack Mabry came into the saloon. When they had ordered their drinks, Dixon asked, "Where's Tune?"

"Having himself a bath, a shearing and a shave," Keno said.

The four Anchor men drank in silence, their faces revealing the gravity of their thoughts. Finally Dixon asked, "How come Spade licked you galoots so quick?"

"Licked us?" Big Joe Walsh said. "Hell, we ain't started to fight yet."

"You mean Anchor isn't finished?" Dixon asked hopefully.

Walsh peered at him in feigned astonishment. "Whatever gave you that notion?" he asked.

And Keno Smith said, "We just been dawdling around, waiting to git our dander up. We ain't really mad yet. But we're getting close to it."

Tracey Fayette had seen Tune early this morning when he and Keno came in for breakfast. Both men were groggy from lack of sleep, and Tune had looked the worst she had ever seen him—like a grotesque charicature of himself. He had lost weight, his eyes were bloodshot and his gaunt, scarred face was darkly shagged with a stubble of whiskers.

Her first reaction had been anger that a man would subject himself to such abuse. She had twitted him about June Patterson's visit, saying the woman had reported him in good health. But Tune had dredged up his old self-mocking smile and told her how nice she looked, and then she had felt sorry for him.

There had been little opportunity to talk, what with other customers and the fact that Keno was with him. All day she had looked forward to seeing him at supper, but now it was near closing time and he hadn't shown up. She wondered if he had eaten supper at the hotel, if perhaps he was angry because of her mention of June Patterson.

Tracey pulled down the front window blinds. But she didn't close the door. Instead, she stood in the doorway, peering at the street and feeling guilty because she so wanted to see him. Lew Tune, she told herself, would never change; he would go on being what he was for the rest of his life. It was silly, she thought, to be so concerned about him.

Tom Greer came from the kitchen wearing his battered old hat and shabby coat. With his usual pessimism he said, "Another day nearer the end. Better turn out the lights or you'll have more customers."

"Good night, Tom," Tracey said, and watched him hobble toward Faro Charlie's Saloon, his peg leg thumping the plank walk. There, she thought, goes what's left of a gunfighter. Perhaps he had once been like Lew Tune—a reckless, hell-for-leather, easy-laughing man; now he was old, cranky and crippled with a saloon for a refuge when his day's work was done.

Turning away from the door, Tracey put out one of the bracket lamps, then returned to the doorway—and saw him coming. She told herself that she shouldn't stand there, waiting for him like a silly schoolgirl. But she did. And when he came in she said frankly, "I've been waiting for you, Lew."

"Had to get a haircut," he said. He took off his hat and ducked his head toward her and said, "Don't I smell nice now?"

Tracey ignored the hair tonic. She fingered the scar that grooved his cheek and said in a subdued voice, "So awfully close."

Following her into the kitchen, Tune took a chair at the table and reflected, "I'm getting to be a regular kitchen customer."

Tracey brought his food and poured him a cup of coffee. She said, "I'm sorry it turned out the way it did, but I'm glad it's over."

Tune began eating. Presently he said, "It's not over."

"But Anchor is gone, and they say Tilt Isham may be dying."

Tune shrugged. "Tilt is still alive. So am I. So are Keno, Big Joe Walsh, Jack Mabry and Pete Maroney."

"What chance would that many men have against Spade's big crew?" Tracey asked.

"Not much in a head-to-head fight. But we're going after them Injun style—real sneaky."

Tune ate hurriedly, and Tracey asked, "Why all the rush?"

"We're riding out, soon as I finish," he said. Then he asked, "Have you seen Jim Beam lately?"

"He was in day before yesterday. Jim told me you had to leave his place because of Cameron's orders."

Tune nodded. "Jim doesn't like chancy deals. He wants security—peace and quiet." Afraid that it sounded like criticism, he added, "It's the way he's made. Jim can't help that, any more than I can help the way I'm made."

"You like to fight, don't you?" Tracey suggested.

Tune shook his head. "But I can't abide being pushed around."

Tracey poured him another cup of coffee. She asked, "With Anchor gone, where will you eat and sleep?"

As if thinking this out, Tune said slowly, "We'll eat where we find food, I guess. And sleep in the brush."

Tracey was silent for a long moment while she watched him finish his supper. Then she said suddenly, "Oh, Jim —can't you see that it's useless to keep on fighting? Can't you accept defeat? Why continue a lost cause that can end only with you getting killed?"

Surprised at the emotion in her voice and the look of near tears in her eyes, Tune said, "Maybe this doesn't make sense to you, Tracey. You're a woman—you don't understand how a man feels about a thing like this. But I'm not quitting."

"Not even if I plead with you?" Tracey insisted. "If I say you mean so much to me that I can't stand seeing you killed, or horribly wounded?"

That astonished Tune, and bewildered him. "Why would you care that much?" he asked. "It's Jim you're marrying, not me."

"Perhaps I'm not going to marry Jim," she said quietly.

Tune studied her lamplit face, finding no clue in her composed features, or in her unwavering eyes. He asked, "Has Jim done something wrong—something to make you change your mind?"

Tracey shook her head. "He's done nothing. Maybe that's it. While you've been fighting, he's been standing idly by. And he allowed Cameron to tell him you couldn't stay at his place after all you did for him."

Tune remained silent, not knowing what to say. Women, he supposed, were never very consistent where emotions were involved. Her reaction made no sense to him. On the one hand she was blaming him for fighting Cameron, yet she was blaming Jim Beam for not fighting Cameron.

As he got up, Tracey moved close to him and said urgently, "Don't go, Lew—don't get yourself killed."

Tune took her in his arms. He looked into her tear-spangled eyes, marveling at the womanly warmth of them, and at her lips, so red and gently smiling now. The pressure of her arms did something to him, and told him something, so that he knew what he had only guessed before—she had a full woman's need for a man of her own choosing, she was like a brimming glass filled to overflowing. When he kissed her she was eagerly receptive, wholly responsive, and for this moment nothing else had substance or meaning; there was no reality beyond this selfless merging that gripped them in a tight-clamped fist of man-woman awareness.

When finally she drew back, dazed and breathless, Tune asked, "Did I tell you that you're the only woman I ever loved?"

Tracey shook her head.

"Well, it's true. You're the only one."

"Darling," she whispered. Her arms tightened around him and she murmured, "I'll never let you go."

For a moment then, with the remembered sweetness of her lips, and the perfumed, woman scent of her a continuing fragrance, Tune was tempted to renege on his promise to Tilt Isham. In that moment, comparing what he had here with what awaited him out there on the lonely trails, he couldn't do it. There was more than a promise involved; there was Bart Hayden. . . .

He said, "It won't be for long, I promise you."

"But you don't have to go, Lew. It's your choice to make."

He shook his head. "The choice was made before I came in here, Tracey."

She wasn't smiling now. She looked at him with an expression of disbelief, and when she spoke, her throaty, low-toned voice held a reserve and a note of self-reproach. "I thought being with me—we two together—would be enough. But I must have been wrong."

"No, you weren't wrong," Tune said, searching for words to make her understand. "It's just that I've got to finish this deal. I've got to stop Spade's steer herd from reaching town—and I've got to settle my score with Bart Hayden. Don't you see, Tracey? I couldn't live here without doing that."

"We could live somewhere else," she said. "You could start over again."

"Not until I finish this deal," he said flatly.

Tracey pulled away from him. She said, "All right. Go

out there and get yourself killed." Her eyes filled with tears. She wiped them away with her apron and cried angrily, "You're stupid, Lew Tune—plain stupid!"

He moved toward her, wanting to comfort her, to make her understand. But she turned away from him, and now her eyes flashed with the intensity of her feeling as she said, "I'd never marry a stupid man. Never."

Tune picked up his hat. He said, "Well, thanks for a fine meal." As he went to the door, Tracey said insistently, "Don't you talk Jim into joining your fight against Spade."

Tune opened the door. He asked, "A good-bye kiss?"

For a moment he thought she would come to him. The anger faded from her eyes and the pressure at the corners of her mouth relaxed so that her lips were softly curved as if on the point of smiling. But she shook her head, and then the anger returned, and she said, "I don't kiss stupid men."

She was like that, her oval face angry and scornful, when Tune went out and closed the door behind him.

Half an hour later Tune rode out of town with Smith, Walsh and Mabry. Their saddlebags were crammed with provisions, extra cartridges and utensils. As they rode past Fancy Mayme's place, Big Joe Walsh said, "There's a red-headed gal in there I sure like a lot. One of these days me and her might get married."

"June Patterson?" Tune asked.

"Yeah—used to be a waitress at the Acme. She cottons to me. Calls me Biggy for short. By God, she's what I call a real double-breasted woman."

"I knowed a whore like that in Denver once," Keno Smith said. "She made a man feel seven foot tall."

"June ain't no whore, correctly speaking," Big Joe explained. "She's a waitress by trade."

Presently Tune said, "The first thing we've got to do is find the steer herd."

"And after that?" Mabry inquired.

Before Tune could reply, Keno Smith said, "Why, we'll pat each steer on the forehead and say, 'Primoroso vaca.'"

"What does that mean?" Mabry asked.

"Nice cow," Keno said.

CHAPTER 21

NEWS of Anchor's fall had spread through the Hoodoo Hills, and with it came word that Spade was in control of the entire range. Homesteaders and greasy-sack nesters got the word from victory-flushed Spade riders who inquired about Anchor men hiding out in the hills. The small outfits had no love for Anchor. Through the frequent forays of Whitey Melotte, the big outfit had lorded it over them for years, but they understood that these gun-hung Spade toughs would be even less charitable.

Indian Joe Spears kept tight-lipped about his night excursion to Reservation and the cargo he had carried. This secrecy was not prompted by any sense of loyalty to Tilt Isham, but by fear of reprisal from Riley Cameron.

While their men roamed the hills watching nester outfits and water holes, Cameron and Hayden took their ease at Beam's place. They had obtained a keg of whiskey from Indian Joe and were in a boozy state of exhilaration on this third day after the Willow Spring fight.

"This, by God, is how it's going to be from now on—plenty booze, plenty range and plenty cash," Riley bragged expansively. "Me and you, we got this country in our hip pocket."

A dozen men were camped near the corrals; their number increased as other men rode in and unsaddled. They had their own supper fire going, while Jim Beam cooked supper for Cameron and Hayden in the shack.

Now, as another man rode in, Cameron hailed him. "Have a drink on Spade," he invited. "Any sign of them bastards?

"Nary a sign," the rider said. He took his drink at the keg and led his horse to the corral.

"They can't hole up forever," Cameron said confidently. "They got to eat, and we know one is wounded from the bandages we found."

"Do you suppose they doubled back toward Willow Spring," Hayden suggested. "That would be a smart move. We've only got four men there."

Jim Beam came out of the shack with a butcher knife and walked to where a yearling carcass hung suspended from a tree. He carved three steaks and came back across the darkening yard. The two partners, lounging in the dust, paid him no heed, but Beam said flatly, "I'll expect to be paid for that yearling."

Cameron chuckled. He said to Hayden, "Sounds downright unsociable to me."

"Inhospitable," Hayden said. "Couple neighbors drop in for supper and the man expects them to pay for the beef they eat."

Jim Beam had bowed to the necessity of having his place taken over by Spade riders. He had told himself, *Wait it out.* But his resentment had grown with each day's passing and now he had reached the end of his restraint.

"I want pay for the yearling, inhospitable or not," he said, and went into the shack.

Hayden got up, refilled his tin cup at the keg and walked into the shack. He said, "Don't get touchy with us, friend Beam. We're the big outfit here now."

"That's right," Cameron said, joining his partner at the table. "Them that string along with us can run cattle in this country—them that don't are through."

The steaks were frying now. That smell, combined with the fine flavor of simmering frijoles and boiling coffee made an appetizing odor that whetted Cameron's hunger. He had, he thought, everything a man would want—good food, whiskey, plenty of riders, and a sweet-loving woman waiting for him at the ranch. This was what twenty years of waiting and conniving had brought him. He was the Big Mogul. . . .

Tune and his three companions ate breakfast at Gil Morgan's ranch that morning. This was a roundabout way of getting to their destination, but Tune thought it might be the best way; by-passing the region where Spade riders were most likely to be, they could come into the Hoodoo Hills from the southwest and angle east to Willow Spring.

Morgan fed them well, and wished them well, but he didn't offer to join them when the took off. Afterward, Keno Smith remarked, "He hates Hayden's guts and has no use for Riley Cameron, but he won't blast a cap against them."

At noon they stopped at a seep on the western shank of the Hoodoos, high enough so that the air was crisp. After eating, they rested for two hours, then continued the climb through an almost impassable canyon. This, Tune thought, was the hard way to get where they were going; but because Spade wouldn't suspect this approach, he was reasonably sure of reaching Willow Spring without a fight. From now on that would be a primary factor of his strategy—to avoid a clash with Spade riders. Four men might stop the steer herd, if they kept at it, day after day; the loss of a man, or two men, would ruin their chances.

They rimmed out of the canyon shortly before sundown and camped in a desolate region of weather-carved rock reefs where wind-twisted pinons clung precariously to the flinty soil. It was a dry camp and, because of the elevation, a cold one. All hands foraged for firewood, but the result of their combined efforts was not enough to keep a fire going until midnight.

"When the moon comes up, we'll ride," Tune decided.

Three hours later they were asaddle again, picking their way through jumbled boulders that glinted in the frosty moonight. . . .

Another day of riding brought them to the pine-clad ridge above Willow Spring. There was no sign of activity at the line camp, where two horses dozed in the corral. But farther out on the flats to the west a considerable number of cattle grazed.

"Two herders yonder," Keno Smith said.

Tune had not observed them, but presently located one rider sitting his horse beyond the far fringes of the herd.

"Where's the other one?" he asked.

"On that little knoll about five miles north," Keno said.

Tune marveled at Smith's eyesight. After peering north for an interval, he said, "I'll take your word for it."

A slight breeze was blowing off the flats, bringing the combined odors of dust and sun-cured grass and cow droppings. Fall had turned the grass tawny, and tinted the leaves of willows clustered about the springs; farther off, a line of cottonwoods along a creek bed looked like orderly stacks of cured hay.

"What do we do now?" Jack Mabry asked.

"Loaf," Tune said. "And wait."

"Wait for what?"

"For Spade to start driving those steers."

Tune led his companions along the ridge and then down to a spring in a canyon some eight miles west of the line camp. Here they unsaddled, hobbled their horses and made a fire for their coffeepots. Later, just before sundown, Tune rode back to the pines and had his look at the line camp, waiting until the two day herders came in for supper. Then, observing two more men, he thought, *Night herders*.

The waiting continued for another day and night without the arrival of Cameron's big crew. The next day Tune suggested that Keno and Big Joe ride to Spade's North Camp and garner some provisions. "I don't think there'll be anyone there," he said. "If there is, be damned sure you don't tangle with them."

The two rode off leading Mabry's saddled pony, which would be used for a packhorse. Mabry didn't like it; he said, "I'll be afoot if something happens."

"No," Tune said. "My pony will tote double real good."

It was after midnight when Smith and Walsh returned with an assortment of canned goods, staples and a quarter of beef lashed to the led pony. Unsaddling in the moonlight, Keno said, "Now we can live high off the hog."

They did, waiting two more days. Then, near noon of the following day, Spade's crew arrived and began rounding up the steers. "They'll have a trail herd shaped by tomorrow morning," Tune predicted.

"I think there's a change of weather coming," Keno prophesied. "My broke shoulder is aching."

There wasn't a cloud in the sky. But knowing Keno's ability as a weather forecaster, Tune said, "A storm might make our job easier."

Sometime during the night a cold wind blowing against his face awakened Tune. A great bank of high-riding clouds hid the moon, and he thought, *Keno was right*. He had deliberately banished Tracey Fayette from his mind, but now, listening to the rising wind, he remembered her refusal to understand why he had to go on with the fight against Spade. He could forgive her for that, for she was a woman with a woman's inability to reason like a man. But he couldn't forgive her scathing accusation that he was stupid, nor the scornful way she had refused to kiss him good-bye.

Later, just before he went back to sleep, Tune remembered how it was with her snugged in his arms; how receptive and eager she had been. . . .

Riley Cameron had discarded his expansive mood of boozy good-fellowship; he drove his crew with the urgency of a man racing against time. Eying the accumulating clouds that blanked out the sun at midmorning, he said to Bart Hayden, "We're in for a storm. I want this drive started within another hour."

It was, with the lead steers passing the line camp shortly after eleven o'clock. Riding point with Cameron, Hayden asked, "Do we head straight east across Apache Flats to the Anchor road?"

"Hell, no," Cameron said. "We take the short route through the Hoodoos."

A blustering wind, rank and cold, came out of the west. It began to rain about the time the trail herd veered into the hills. Shivering riders cursed as they donned slickers; spooky steers broke from the herd and were chased by morose men who wondered why they had ever taken up this way of earning a living.

The slanting rain and low-hovering clouds lessened visibility to near darkness. The long file of steers was plodding up a shallow, brush-fringed arroyo when guns began blasting about midway of the herd.

"Goddamn!" Riley Cameron exclaimed.

And Bart Hayden, clawing a Winchester from saddle scabbard, shouted, "There's your hideout bastards!"

The firing didn't last long, but it effectively split the herd into two segments. One batch of steers stampeded east, crashing through brush in high-tailed flight, while the remainder of the herd doubled back on itself, creating a mad tangle of rain-pelted confusion.

The odd part of it was that no Spade rider sighted an attacker, during the outburst of firing or afterward.

Two steers were dead in the trail, the others were scattered in all directions. Afterward, when darkness ended the work of gathering cattle, fully half the crew remained asaddle, circling the chuck wagon, while the other half ate a rain-splattered supper.

"Those bastards couldn't have picked a worse time to hit us," Cameron complained.

It took most of the following day to get the steers gathered into a trail herd. The rain turned to sleet the next morning, and tempers were edgy as the crew cursed the steers into motion. Because nearly half his riders were acting as guards on either side of the trail, Cameron was short-handed with the herd.

Some time after noon a gun began blasting near the head of the column; that rain-muffled disturbance attracted the guards, who came galloping through the mud. Soon after that other guns let loose near the middle of the herd, causing a stampede that was almost identical with the first one. The difference was that a Spade rider received a broken leg when his horse went down, and there were five dead steers in the trail instead of two.

When it was over, with the attackers melting into the sleety gloom without a shot having been fired at them, Riley Cameron was like a raving maniac. "We've been jumped twice and not one of you blind bastards has seen a single son of a bitch—much less shot one!" he raged. "In three days we've come less than fifteen miles!"

"At the rate we're going we'll be lucky to reach Reservation by spring," Bart Hayden muttered.

It got worse instead of better. In the next three days they were hit twice and made practically no mileage. . . .

All that rain-drenched week, while Spade spent half the time gathering stampeded steers, Tune and his companions kept up a steady harassment. Twice they made night attacks, firing into the camp from four directions, then regrouping at a prearranged bivouac. Spade endeavored to trail them, but Tune's raiders never used the same camping place twice. Misery camps they were, with never enough food or blankets, never enough sleep. But at the end of the second week, the steers had not reached Tailholt.

Wild rumors spread through the hills, and some of them reached Reservation. Two Spade riders, one with a broken leg, came into town with the fantastic story that half of Cameron's big crew had been killed. They stayed only long enough to have Doc Snyder set and splint the broken leg, then caught the first stage east.

Three Spade riders drifted in a few days later, telling of an all-out fight. They, too, took the first stage out of town. The next day Jack Mabry rode in supporting Big Joe Walsh in saddle. Walsh had a bullet in the back, and Mabry, with a deep chest cold, was on the verge of having pneumonia. When June Patterson heard about Big Joe, she came to the hotel and volunteered to be his nurse.

Two days later Tate Engle, his son Jeddy and the Mexican woman, Maria, arrived with the story that Spade headquarters had been burned to the ground.

This news cheered Sheriff Dixon, who made it a point to call on Tilt Isham that afternoon. Anchor's boss was still bedfast, but he was slowly regaining his strength and was considered out of danger. He voiced his confidence in Tune by saying, "I chose the right man to ramrod this fight."

Later, having supper with Faro Charlie at the Acme, Dixon bragged, "It looks like I picked the right side, after all."

"Thanks to Lew Tune," the saloonman said sourly. "That rank Injun don't know when to quit. Never saw a man like him."

Overhearing that declaration, Tracey Fayette was in wholehearted agreement. For three weeks she had been expecting the worst each time someone rode in from the Hoodoo Hills, her dread growing with each dreary day's passing. Faro Charlie had described Lew Tune exactly: he was rank, and he didn't know when to quit. And, between anger and tears, she thought, *There's never been a man like him.*

CHAPTER 22

THE snow began as big wet flakes sifting gently down on the windless, rain-soaked hills at dawn while Lew Tune crouched over a feeble campfire. Keno Smith sat under an improvised tent fashioned from tree branches and a slicker. "This camping out on short rations gets tiresome after a while, Lew. What say we go into town and have us a few drinks?"

"Not me, but it's time you went in," Tune said. As they ate breakfast, he explained, "This is the last of our grub." He glanced at the two slat-ribbed ponies standing dejectedly nearby, and added, "We're damn near afoot."

Smith grunted agreement. He blew on his coffee, complaining, "It's weak as a sick woman's sweat, and hotter'n hog scald."

Presently Tune said, "We've used up Jim Beam's horses, and most of his provisions. Cameron has taken over Indian Joe's store, so that's out. It looks like you'll have to go to town."

"Why not both of us?" Keno asked. "We've earned a vacation."

Tune shook his head. "In this going it'll take nearly two days to get there. And if this snow continues, it'll take longer than that to come back. Maybe a week all told. I don't want to leave Spade alone that long."

"But they've give up trying to drive steers, Lew. All they're doing now is chasing us around these goddamn hills."

Tune ignored that. He said, "I've got nine horses at the

livery. You can ride one and lead three, and tote us some supplies. Come to Beam's place by way of the Anchor road and Lost Horse camp. I'll meet you there."

Keno rubbed his left shoulder. "That old break is giving me the miseries," he said. "We're due for a big storm."

"You can get some liniment in town," Tune suggested. "Also bring back a bottle of bourbon. No telling when we might get bitten by a rattlesnake."

The mention of whiskey brightened Keno's eyes. "I'd like to go on a hell-tootin' spree," he mused. "It would cure all my aches and pains."

Afterward, as Smith rode off through the snow, Tune thought, *He's liable to do just that.*

He packed up his gear and rode into the mealy gloom, allowing the underfed bay pony to set its own pace. This had been a hard week on grass-fed horses, for they had been ridden far distances in the worst kind of muddy going. Thinking of the long trek to Spade headquarters, Tune grimaced. He hadn't enjoyed what had gone on there—the shooting of two men, nor the burning of the ranch afterward. Remembering the Mexican woman's hysterical weeping and Tate Engle's bewilderment, Tune wondered what Tracey Fayette would think when she heard about it. And she'd hear, once the survivors reached Reservation.

The snowflakes were smaller now, and the air colder. Wind lashed the pine tops to a continued swishing, and Tune thought, *This could turn into a blizzard.* He was headed for Jim Beam's place; crossing the main trail west of Tailholt, he stopped for a moment to study the tracks here.

Spade, he saw, was on the hunt again, for several riders had passed this way since dawn. Observing cattle browsing on brush, he identified them as part of Spade's ill-fated steer herd. Those steers were a symbol of his success. He had promised Tilt Isham to stop them, and by God he had. Cameron had taken his chuck wagon into Tailholt, thereby admitting his drive was stopped. Spade's boss was using Indian Joe's store as a base for his hunting expedition.

Tune was a mile north of the trail when a rider loomed up directly ahead of him. They fired at almost the same moment, the Spade rider's hastily aimed bullet missing Tune by a foot or more, but Tune's slug knocked down the other man's horse. He saw the rider dive clear, rolling over and over in the snow. Almost at once a man farther west yelled out, and Tune was wheeling away from that sound when a man south of him shouted, "Come up—come up!"

Tune changed course again, but a moment later a rider came charging out of the snow haze so close that he identified Riley Cameron. Spade's boss got in the first shot, that bullet snarling past Tune's left shoulder. He fired at Cameron, who had jerked his horse sideways into thicket that momentarily screened him. Cameron lost his hat; he yelled again, "Come up—come up!"

Tune angled around, firing and missing, and seeing Cameron's snow-dusted monk's fringe of rusty hair duck as he aimed another shot. A wind-raveled voice called, "Riley, where you at?"

"Over here!" Cameron shouted, and fired again.

That slug burned across Tune's right thigh. Taking a steady aim, he squeezed off a shot and saw Cameron jerk back. He fired again, and then, as Cameron fell, spurred his pony to headlong flight.

A man came up on his left, asking, "Is that you, Riley?"

Tune grinned, knowing that he had all the best of it; in this snow-swirled gloom Spade riders couldn't be sure who they were firing at. But he could be sure. As he kept going, the man fired, that bullet pinking the bay's rump and propelling him to a frantic, faster run.

There was another shot, and more wind-borne voices. But they were all behind him now and Tune thought, *I'm a fool for luck.*

Later he swung back to the trail, merging his pony's tracks with the others there. The wind was blowing harder now, and the snow was beginning to drift; in another hour there would be no sign of a trail. Tune turned north again, traveling for upwards of five miles before quartering east toward Beam's place. So cold now that his teeth were chattering, Tune dismounted and trudged through the snow beside his horse. At first his wounded leg was numb, but presently it began to ache and there was a feeling of warm wetness that ran down to his foot.

Later, riding through snow-pelted semidarkness, Tune thought, *Not fit for man nor beast.* But then he realized that it had been a big day for him, and for Tilt Isham. Riley Cameron was dead. . . .

Bart Hayden had argued against going out on the hunt this morning. He had said, "They'll hole up today, waiting for it to stop snowing. We should do the same."

But Riley Cameron, beside himself with rage and frustration, wouldn't listen. "We can't move steers until we chop down them Anchor bastards," he insisted. "We've got to hunt 'em, snow or no snow."

"Suit yourself," Hayden told him. "But I'm staying close to the fire today."

Now, as Spade's remaining four riders filed into the store late in the afternoon, Hayden asked sarcastically, "How many Anchor men did you catch today?"

Ignoring his question, the four snow-powdered riders strode to the bar and ordered drinks.

Presently Hayden inquired, "Where's Riley?"

"Out back," a man said.

The four held their glasses in cold-numbed fingers. As the store's heat thawed them out, they opened their mackinaws. But they didn't talk.

Hayden heaved another log onto the fire. Listening to the wind, he said. "This is going to be a good night to be under cover." Then he asked, "What's Riley doing out back?"

"Why, he's doing exactly nothing," a man said.

"What you mean?" Hayden demanded.

"I mean Riley's dead—stiff as a mackerel."

Hayden got up from his comfortable perch before the fireplace. He asked, "Did you run into Tune?"

"Riley did, I guess. He caught two slugs in the chest."

Hayden came to the bar and ordered a drink. Indian Joe poured it before asking, "If Cameron is dead, who's going to pay for all the whiskey and food?"

"I am," Hayden said. There was a plain note of satisfaction in his voice when he added, "I'm owner of Spade now, and I'll give the orders."

A bearded giant of a man known as Kid Curley, growled, "You'll give me no orders."

"Why won't I?" Hayden demanded.

Kid Curly looked him in the eye. He said, "I wasn't overly fond of Cameron, but I can't stomach you at all. I'm pulling out in the morning."

At about this same time, Lew Tune rode into Jim Beam's snow-swirled yard, marveling at how cheerful and inviting the shack's lamplit windows looked. Going on to the barn, he unsaddled and forked the bay a big feed of hay. Then he limped to the shack's door, and opening it, announced, "The bad penny has turned up—again."

"You're just in time for supper," Beam said. Genuinely

pleased, he added, "I was thinking about you, Lew—wishing you'd pay me a visit."

Tune limped to the stove, took off his gloves and held his hands to the fire. "Damn, it's cold out there," he said, and stood for an interval before shedding his mackinaw.

Beam noticed that he was limping, and now observed the melting blood on his pant leg. "So you got hit," he said.

"Just a slashed muscle is all. Riley Cameron. But he won't shoot anyone else."

"You killed him?" Beam asked.

Tune nodded.

Beam, stirring a pot of stew on the stove, peered at him in round-eyed wonderment. He said thoughtfully, "Then it's over, Lew. The fight is finished."

"Just about," Tune agreed. He sat down and made a cigarette before adding, "The steer drive has been stopped, and most of Spade's crew has vamoosed, I reckon."

"How about Bart Hayden?"

"He's next," Tune said, "and I know where to find him. Maybe tomorrow."

"Indian Joe's?"

Tune nodded.

He ate a bounteous supper, then shed his pants and lay on the bunk while Beam cleaned and bandaged the deep gash on his thigh. Afterward, listening to the wind howl while Beam washed the supper dishes, Tune reflected drowsily, "This would have been a bad one to sleep out in." Soon after that he fell into a deep sleep.

CHAPTER **23**

IT had stopped snowing during the night, but the wind was still blowing when Tune went out to feed the horses. His right leg felt stiff, and it ached when he walked, but otherwise he felt good after a night of dreamless sleep.

They ate a leisurely breakfast. Afterward, with a cigarette and a second cup of coffee, Tune said, "I'd like to spend the day in here just loafing by the fire."

"Why don't you?" Beam asked.

"Well, I'm pretty sure where Hayden is today. Tomorrow he might be gone—ramming around in the hills."

Beam watched him get into his mackinaw; he said, "This might not turn out so good, if there's other men with Hayden."

"Not more than two or three," Tune estimated. "I'll take my chances with them, to get a shot at Hayden."

Beam was ill at ease. He kept tinkering with his shirt, buttoning and unbuttoning it. As Tune took out his pistol and checked its loads, Beam said, "I've always been somewhat of a coward, Lew."

That surprised Tune. In all his life he had never heard a man make that admission. "It's just the way a man is made," he said. "Some like to fight, some don't."

"No, it's more than that. I wanted to fight when Cameron's crew took over my place. But I didn't have the guts to stand up to him."

As if thinking this out, he added, "A man can't spend his whole life dodging fights. He has to make a stand sometime."

"Suppose," Tune agreed, and put on his hat.

He was limping toward the door when Beam said solemnly, "I'm going with you."

Tune turned, asked, "Why?"

"To help even the odds," Beam said. "By God, I can't let you face this alone. This one time I'm going to side you."

Tune shrugged. Then abruptly he remembered what Tracey Fayette had said about not having Beam join the fight against Spade. Whereupon he said, "I guess not, Jim. I'll not be gunning for those other men—just Hayden. Him and me."

"I'll come along, just in case," Beam said.

Still remembering Tracey's words, Tune muttered, "No, you'd only be in the way."

It was like a slap in the face to Jim Beam. At this moment he looked utterly ashamed—as dejected as a man could be. But he said stubbornly, "I'm coming, regardless."

They saddled up and rode out of the yard, not speaking as their ponies scuffed through fetlock-deep snow. The wind had a cutting edge; it penetrated their mackinaws and flung loose snow in their faces.

This, Tune thought, was an odd situation. For the first time Jim Beam was riding with him on a gunfight mission. He guessed now that Jim's conscience had been bothering him these past weeks, that Jim had been torn between his wish for peaceful living and a need to be loyal.

Later, when they rode through timber where the wind

didn't get at them, Tune said, "I promised Tracey I wouldn't pull you into this deal, Jim. That's why I said you'd be in the way."

Beam peered at him, studying his face as if wanting to be sure this was the truth. Then he smiled and said, "That makes it better, Lew—a whole lot better."

Bart Hayden had scraped frost from a front window and now watched Kid Curley and another man ride away from Indian Joe's store. "Good riddance," he muttered, and joined the two remaining Spade riders in front of the fire. He knew them only as Tex, a horse-faced, lathy individual, and Shorty, a neckless, round-shouldered chunk of a man.

Indian Joe was in the kitchen, preparing a noon meal. Hayden went behind the bar and poured three drinks. "A precaution against frostbite," he announced. He raised his glass and offered a toast, saying, "Consternation to our enemies."

"Such as Tune?" Shorty inquired.

"Especially Tune. That bastard has been bad luck to me all the way from Sonora. But now things have changed. What he did yesterday was all in my favor. Instead of owning half of Spade, I own it all."

Tex eyed him gravely; he asked, "Then you're glad Riley is dead?"

"No, not that. But it turned out in my favor."

Hayden began pouring another round of drinks. He was like that, bottle in hand, when Lew Tune yanked the door open and stepped quickly inside, followed by Jim Beam.

Hayden hurled the bottle at Tune, the drew his gun and ducked behind the counter. Tune fired, that shot smashing a glass on the bar top. Tex had drawn his gun, whirling and firing. Jim Beam fired at this same instant, and Tex folded at the middle like a loosely filled sack of grain.

Shorty yelled, "I'm out of it!" and raised both hands.

Now Hayden fired and a bullet lanced along Tune's left side, but he paid it no heed as he swerved to the bar's end for a clean shot at Hayden.

Indian Joe had come to the kitchen doorway. "Stop it!" he screamed in a high, nasal voice. "Stop it, I say!"

Hayden was crouched behind the bar. He bobbed up, looking for Tune, who was now rounding the bar. He fired at Tune hurriedly and inaccurately, then went into a crablike squat as Tune slammed two fast shots at him. Hayden's face was contorted with pain and rage as he tilted up his gun; he blurted, "Goddamn you, Tune," and triggered a shot that splintered the bar.

Tune drove another bullet into him and watched him go altogether slack. Then, while a backwash of tension washed through him, Tune stood unmoving. Here, he thought, was the end of it. For the first time in months he was free of the need to fight.

Indian Joe complained bitterly, "Every time you come here you turn this store into a slaughterhouse. And you leave your messes for me to clean up."

Tune grinned at him. He said, "You're a businessman, Joe. You get the trade—you have to expect some messes."

Jim Beam stood waggling his gun at Shorty, his face pale and tight with tension. He asked nervously, "Did you kill Hayden?"

Tune nodded. He stepped over the dead Tex and lifted Shorty's gun from holster. Then he said to Beam, "You evened the odds, for a fact."

Jim Beam didn't speak. But for the first time since Tune had known him, he looked proud. Really proud.

Keno Smith was enjoying himself. Bellied up to Faro Charlie's bar, he bought a round of drinks for Frank Paddock, Tate Engle and Sheriff Dixon. "It'll all over but the shouting," he said. "Cameron's steer herd is bogged down and most of his crew has quit. Just a matter of me and Lew cleaning up the remnants, is all."

Dixon said, "That's great, Keno. Great. It looked bad for Anchor at one time, but now things have gone the other way."

"And you can keep your star," Faro Charlie said sarcastically.

It was past ten o'clock when Tate Engle said, "Guess I better go to bed. You coming, Frank?"

Paddock nodded. They were partway to the door when Lew Tune came in and asked, "Anybody want a drink?"

Keno loosed a rebel yell. He exclaimed, "Speak of the devil!"

Tune came up to the bar and said to Faro Charlie, "The drinks are on me. We've licked Spade."

"You mean—is Riley Cameron dead?" Dixon asked.

Tune nodded. "So is Hayden. It's all over."

"Damn my knobby knees!" Keno exulted. "You done it all alone?"

126

"Not exactly," Tune said. "Jim Beam threw in with me against Hayden and the two men he had left."

For a moment then, as if having difficulty in absorbing the fact that the long fight was finished, they stood silent. Then Keno asked, "Where's Beam?"

"He left me at the livery, to call on Tracey Fayette."

Frank Paddock asked, "Do we get our cows back—me and Tate?"

Tune nodded. "June Patterson also," he said.

"I got to go tell Tilt Isham the good news," Dixon said, and hurried from the saloon.

Tune raised his glass. "Drink up, boys," he invited. "We've got some celebrating to do."

They were on their third round when Jim Beam came in. He was greeted jovially as one of the gang, and Keno Smith bragged, "You took my place while I was gone, which is a considerable chore for any man to tackle."

But Beam's face was entirely grave as he said, "Lew, there's someone outside wants to see you."

"Me?" Tune said, and guessing who it was, asked, "You sure?" Beam nodded, whereupon Tune limped to the door and opened it and saw Tracey Fayette standing on the stoop. She wore a long coat, but no hat, and her hair was dusted with snowflakes.

"Lew!" she said, and came into his arms at once.

Holding her tight, with the fragrance of her hair a well-remembered perfume, Tune said, "You told me you wouldn't marry a stupid man."

"I know," she said. As if accusing him of things beyond forgiveness, she said, "You're stupid, and rank as an Indian. You don't know when to quit."

The cold air was clearing the whiskey haze from Tune's brain, but even so this made no sense to him. "Then why are you here?" he asked.

"Because," she said.

Inside, Keno Smith let loose with another rebel yell; there was the door-muffled sound of loud talk and laughter.

"Because why?"

"I can't help it, Lew—I just can't help it."

Night's coldness stained her cheeks; in the half-light here her face was a smooth oval loveliness, gently smiling, and she met his gaze directly, allowing him to glimpse the hidden hungers of a woman wholly receptive. She said, in a sighing resigned way, "You'll never change. I know that."

"But I have," Tune insisted. "You've changed me from a shiftless saddle tramp to a man who owns cattle."

She was snugged tight against him, so tight that the superficial wound along his ribs ached from the pressure. He asked, "Would you kiss a stupid man, ma'am?"

Tracey nodded.

Tune delayed for a moment longer, gazing down into her face and being hugely stirred by what he saw there. He said gustily, "The only woman I ever loved."

Then he kissed her with the urgency of a man claiming a priceless possession.

The End